"This morning, two men kidnapped me and Charity."

"You should have gone to the police, Arissa," Nathan said.

"What could they have done? We both know that area—the gangs rule those streets. If this is related to the drug gang that killed my brother, what hope do I have that the police can protect us? And my parents?"

Pain flashed across Nathan's face, and he abruptly stood again. This time he went to lean against the fireplace mantel.

Even after three years, did her brother's death pain him so much? Or maybe it was the memory of the day Nathan's leg had been shattered. She swallowed, remembering what he'd told her about his leg. About how he would never walk again because of her brother. The words still cut.

She took a deep breath. Seeing Nathan again had her caught up in too many memories. What was past should stay there. She hoped Nathan would help her, but she couldn't fool herself into thinking their relationship would ever be anything remotely like it had once been....

Books by Camy Tang

Love Inspired Suspense

Deadly Intent
Formula for Danger
Stalker in the Shadows
Narrow Escape

CAMY TANG

writes romance with a kick of wasabi. Originally from Hawaii, she worked as a biologist for nine years, but now she writes full-time. She is a staff worker for her San Jose church youth group and leads a worship team for Sunday service. She also runs the Story Sensei fiction critique service, which specializes in book doctoring. On her blog, she gives away Christian novels every Monday and Thursday, and she ponders frivolous things like dumb dogs (namely hers), coffee-geek husbands (no resemblance to her own…), the writing journey, Asiana and anything else that comes to mind. Visit her website, www.camytang.com.

NARROW ESCAPE

CAMY TANG

Love Inspired

Recycling programs
for this product may
not exist in your area.

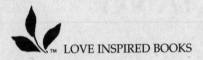 ™ LOVE INSPIRED BOOKS

ISBN-13: 978-0-373-08343-5

NARROW ESCAPE

www.LoveInspiredBooks.com

Printed in U.S.A.

He lifted me out of the slimy pit, out of the mud and mire; he set my feet on a rock and gave me a firm place to stand. He put a new song in my mouth, a hymn of praise to our God. Many will see and fear the LORD and put their trust in him.

—Psalm 40:2–3

Thanks to my Street Team members for helping me with names: Jennifer Fuchikami for naming Arissa and various characters, and Charity Lyman and Holly Magnuson for naming Charity and Mark.

ONE

Arissa Tiong awoke to darkness and the stench of fear. Pain throbbed from a sharp point at the back of her head and radiated forward to pound against the backs of her eyeballs. She drew in a ragged breath and swallowed dust. She stifled a cough against the scratchy nubs of the frilly carpet she lay on.

Where was she? She tried to move and realized her stiff arms were fastened behind her back, and her ankles were tied together. She attempted to straighten her legs and found her feet were tethered to something. She was bound like an animal.

And Charity. Where was Charity? Her heart began to speed up, and each beat felt like a hammer blow to her breastbone. Her entire body ached.

The dim room narrowed into focus before her swimming vision. Slivers of light came from a boarded-up window. Daylight, it was still daytime. They'd taken her sometime in the morning, and she didn't feel she'd been out for that long, so it must have only been a few hours. The rays spilled onto a rusty metal bed frame that held a thin, sagging mattress with no sheets and several dark stains. Her mind shied away from what made those stains.

The smell of mold was almost overpowering, and dust had settled on the thin carpet, pooling in holes and rips across the surface. The walls had dark water stains painted over older water stains.

She didn't realize there was a ringing in her ears until it started to fade and she could hear noises from outside the room. The sharp hard cries of street kids playing a pick-up game in the middle of a road. She made out a word or two here or there. The kids spoke in Tagalog. She was still in Los Angeles, maybe still in the Filipino community where she lived. She hadn't seen the faces of the men who had nabbed her off the street, but if she remained in her neighborhood, they hadn't taken her far.

What had they done with Charity? Her last memory had been seeing the three-year-old's huge dark eyes, her mouth wide open, screaming and reaching for her as Arissa was hauled backward into a van. Had the men left Charity on the street? A three-year-old girl alone on the streets of L.A.? A cold knife blade slid under her rib cage and pricked her heart.

And why had they taken Arissa? She was only an international flight attendant. Her parents owned a tiny grocery store in a low-income Filipino community that barely earned enough to feed and house the four of them in the minuscule apartment above the store. They had nothing anyone would want.

The men must have taken her by mistake, and when they realized it, they'd kill her.

She closed her eyes. No, she had to see if she could get out of here. She *would* get out of here.

Arissa tugged at her hands behind her

back. It felt like tape wrapped around her wrists. She twisted her arms, arched her back. Agony jabbed from her right shoulder—she must have injured it or fallen on it at some point. She gritted her teeth against the pain and pulled down her arms, getting them under her rear end.

She folded her body in half as she scooted her bound hands along the back of her legs toward her feet. Rope secured her crossed ankles, and a line ran into a tiny closet and fastened to the head of a large nail sticking out of the closet wall.

She reached down to see if she could untie her ankles even though her wrists were bound, but the line gave her a better idea. She sat up and drew her legs closer, pulling the rope taut. She set the edge of the duct tape around her wrists against the rope and started sawing back and forth.

It took forever, but soon the rope cut through and created a tear in the layers of duct tape. Then it was easier to saw through the rest and free her hands, ignoring the blood that trickled down the creases in her wrists from the tape and the friction from the rope.

She was about to untie her ankles when boot steps sounded outside the closed door, coming closer. A child's sobbing approached with the steps.

Charity. They had her niece. Arissa wasn't sure whether to feel relieved or terrified.

She dropped back down to the carpet, tucking her hands behind her back again. Hopefully the men wouldn't realize the tape was gone. She settled into the same position she'd been in when she awoke, and shut her eyes.

The metal doorknob rattled as someone unlocked it, then two different footfalls sounded against the carpet—one lighter than the other, but neither were the steps of a child. One of them must have been carrying Charity, whose soft crying erupted into a wail as she saw Arissa on the floor.

"Let her go," growled a man's voice in Tagalog.

Now she could hear Charity's footsteps, followed by tiny hands that wrapped around

Arissa's head and neck. "Aunty Rissa," Charity sobbed. "Wake up, wake up. Why won't you wake up?"

It took every ounce of willpower not to throw her arms around the small trembling body. Arissa kept her eyes shut. Thankfully, Charity's body shielded her face from the two kidnappers.

"Now be quiet," said a second voice in Tagalog, sharper than the other and slightly higher pitched. They were both men, both Filipino.

Charity gave a startled cry of fear, but then her sobs softened and she buried her face in Arissa's hair.

"See, I told you it would make her be quiet," said the sharp voice. The men walked out of the room. "Why'd you bring her, anyway?"

"It would have been better to leave her crying and screaming in the middle of the street?"

He was one of the men who'd grabbed them, then.

"All this trouble," the deeper voice groused.

"If Mark hadn't gotten shot..." The door closed behind him and metal scraped as they locked it again.

Mark? Arissa's brother, Mark? But he'd been killed in the line of duty over three years ago. Why would these men care about his death and kidnap Arissa now?

And would they go after her parents, too, now that they had Arissa and Charity?

She reached out to gather Charity close to her, and the little girl gave a surprised noise. "Shh, shh. We have to be quiet or they'll come back."

"Why did they take us, Aunty Rissa?" Fresh tears trickled down Arissa's neck.

"I don't know. But we have to get out of here, okay?"

The little head nodded against her ear.

Arissa sat up and worked on the rope tying her legs together. It had been knotted tightly but inexpertly. She tore a fingernail trying to loosen the first knot, but after that she was able to undo the other knots quickly.

The window had been boarded up with plywood so that only slits of light shone through, but as she leaned closer, Arissa could see that the drywall securing the boards was brittle and crumbling. She yanked at a plywood board that she was fairly certain hadn't been nailed into a wall stud, and the bottom edge pulled away easily, with white drywall flakes drifting into the dingy carpet. She tried the top of the board, and it drew free.

So that's why the window had been boarded up—cracks splintered out from the glass, radiating from a small hole. A bullet hole. She glanced behind her into the room, and saw a corresponding hole high in the wall next to the closet door.

She shuddered. Growing up in her area of L.A., she'd gotten used to hearing gunshots every night, but she never got used to seeing the damage to buildings, to people.

She tore away as many of the boards from the window as she could and set them quietly on the floor. Outside, the kids playing in the street had moved on, and the empty road echoed with the whisper of cars driving elsewhere nearby. It seemed to drowse in the bright sunlight as drug dealers slept off a busy night and nosy neighbors watched reality TV shows.

There was also nowhere to hide. The street ran in a straight shot in either direction. These small, old houses had postage-stamp front lawns and broken metal fences around the better ones. Only an occasional scraggly tree or decrepit bush. If she ran with Charity, they'd be spotted down the street in an instant. How long could she run with a three-year-old girl in her arms?

What had Mark always said to her? "Distraction evens the odds."

She scanned the room, easier now that it was brighter, and stepped into the empty closet to look up. A square in the gray asbestos-snowlike ceiling pointed to an entry to the attic crawl space.

She used a board to nudge up the panel and slowly, quietly shift it aside to clear the opening. She wasn't tall enough to get to it easily, or to check that it was safe. She'd have to trust there wasn't anything dangerous in there.

Arissa picked up Charity and whispered in her ear, "You have to be brave for me, *nene*. Can you do that?"

The girl hesitated before nodding slowly. She wasn't her father's daughter for nothing.

"I need you to climb up there and be very, very quiet," Arissa said.

"In the dark?" she whispered, her breath coming faster.

"It's not so dark, see?" Arissa stood under the hole and could see faint rays of sunlight coming through a crack in the roof, illuminating the crawl space. "If you stay very quiet, we can get away from the bad men. Okay?"

Charity took a quick breath. "Okay."

Arissa lifted up the girl and she scrambled into the hole. She pushed at her niece's round bottom, covered in her favorite pink stretch pants, to get her over the edge into the attic. There was a soft shuffling, then Charity's large dark eyes stared down at her from the edge of the hole.

"Stand back," Arissa whispered, "and don't make a sound."

Arissa took the longest of the plywood boards and slid it under the flimsy door-knob, propping the other end of the board against the floor. It wouldn't hold them long, but she only needed a few extra seconds.

She grabbed the heaviest of the other boards and took a deep breath, then swung it against the window glass with all her might.

The impact jarred her arms and shoulders and the sound of shattering glass rang in her ears, making them ache. She hit at the shards of glass left in the window, knocking them loose and shoving them outside. She glanced down and around the outside of the house, spying some dented metal trash cans a few feet to the side of the window. In order to make even more noise, she threw the board at them, knocking one down and making the other rattle ominously against the peel-ing paint of the house.

Men's voices sounded outside the bedroom door, and the knob rattled. The door stuck against the board wedged there.

She ran toward the closet and took a flying leap at the hole in the ceiling just as the men began shouldering at the barricaded door with thundering blows. She grabbed at the edge and swung an elbow over with her momentum, then hauled herself up as quickly and quietly as she could. Thank goodness for the hours she spent at the gym in between her flight assignments. She drew in her legs and laid the panel back over the hole just as the men crashed through the door to the bedroom.

"They're gone!" The voice came from the direction of the window.

"Don't just stand there, we have to get them back."

Footsteps raced out of the bedroom, leaving the house. There was a sound of a slamming door, then all was silent.

She waited a few seconds, straining to hear if there was a third man left in the house, but she didn't hear anything, not even the sound of a television or radio. She pushed aside the panel and dropped down. Reaching up her arms for Charity, the girl obediently dangled her legs over the edge, then slid into her aunt's arms.

She stepped through the splintered bedroom door, walking noiselessly into a small hallway. It opened into a dusty living room, with the open front door at one side and a kitchen door at the other. Arissa headed toward the back of the house.

There was a narrow kitchen door with a cobwebby glass panel. Thankfully it wasn't locked. She opened it and let them into an overgrown backyard, strewn with rusting car parts and various pieces of trash. She carefully closed the door behind her, then made for the sagging back fence, which had several loose slats of wood. She wriggled through one of them, followed by Charity.

Then she picked up her niece and ran.

Nathan Fischer opened the front door and saw his dead partner's eyes staring solemnly up at him.

It took him a moment to realize Mark's eyes were in the face of a three-year-old girl, her dark brown curls blowing about her round cheeks in the crisp Sonoma breeze. Then Nathan's gaze shifted to the young woman standing behind the little girl. The foyer tiles under his feet tilted sideways before righting themselves.

Arissa.

She had lost weight. Her high cheekbones stood out more, and her collarbone peeked from the wide-necked blouse she wore. It was her favorite color, a dusky rose that matched her lips. Her eyes bore into his, wide and intent.

"I'm sorry to drop in on you like this, Nathan, but I need your help." Her voice was the same as he remembered it—low, musical, her words carefully enunciated in a way that hinted at a Filipino accent, although she'd been born in the U.S.

"My help?" he heard himself repeat idiotically. Maybe because he was exhausted—he'd pulled a double shift, taking over for one of the other security officers at Glencove Towers whose wife had gone into labor.

Arissa cast a nervous glance around the neighborhood. The gathering darkness had cast the other bungalow-style homes into shadows, but this was a safe, quiet street in downtown Sonoma—there were no monsters here. Something had spooked her badly.

Especially if she'd come to *him,* after the last words he'd spoken to her three years ago.

"Come in." Nathan stood aside and opened the door wider. The little girl caught his attention again. So Arissa had had a child? The girl seemed tall for her age. So much had happened since he'd last seen Arissa.

She stepped into the foyer of Nathan's parents' home and he closed the door behind her, the light from the hallway lamp casting a glow across her almond-milk-colored skin. He caught a thread of rain and roses, and her familiar scent made him have a flashing urge to give her a peck on the cheek, to say, "Hi, honey, how was work?"

He exhaled a sharp breath to dispel the vision. It was the little girl causing this in him, the reminder that he had once had deeper feelings for this woman, had once wanted to have a family with her. The little girl had fooled him into thinking his dream had come true.

His dream would never come true. Certainly not with *this* woman, and now, not with *any* woman.

Arissa looked around at the foyer, at the brightly hand-painted Spanish tile of the floor that contrasted with the antique Victorian hall table holding a lamp with a ruffled shade.

"I've never been here before, although Mark told me about your parents' house," she said. "Are they home?"

"They left about twenty minutes ago to have dinner with some friends. I just came home from work."

Her eyes found his again. "What are you doing now?"

Now that you can't be a narcotics detective anymore. He blinked and looked away, clearing his head of the condemning voice. "I'm head of security at Glencove Towers." Ironically, the job at the high-end condo building paid more than the LAPD.

The surprise flashed across her brown eyes before she smiled. "That's great. I...I worried about you."

Then she looked away, and he inwardly flinched. She'd said those exact words to him three years ago.

"This is Charity." She stroked the head of the quiet child clinging to her leg. "This is…" She swallowed. "This is Mark's daughter."

The news both surprised and relieved him. He clenched his jaw. He had no right to be relieved. "His daughter? But he never told me anything about a…er, girlfriend." If Mark had been about to be a father, wouldn't that have been something he'd have told his partner? Unless Mark hadn't known?

"His girlfriend was Jemma Capuno," Arissa said carefully, gauging his reaction.

"Johnny Capuno's family?" Was Mark's girlfriend connected to a captain in a Filipino drug gang?

"Johnny's sister," Arissa said.

"What happened to Jemma?"

"Do you remember…" Arissa suddenly colored and looked down at Charity. She bit her lip, then took a quick breath and raised her head. "The day you were shot, there was a young girl in the chop shop. A young pregnant girl."

The memory slammed into him like a freight train. Yes, he remembered everything. The gunshots deafening in the enclosed concrete walls, the bullets ricocheting off metal with low screeches. He remembered the young Filipino girl crouched in a corner, her hands over her swollen belly. Her dress had had blue flowers. She'd been very young and very scared. He hadn't known what happened to her after his leg had been shattered by a bullet.

In response to the memory, his aching thigh twinged. "Come into the living room." He had to sit before his knee started shaking with fatigue.

"I'm sorry," Arissa said. "I shouldn't have kept you standing."

"I'm fine now." The words came out harsher than he intended them to. He was as fine as he could ever expect to be with a shattered femur, after almost a dozen surgeries and months of physical therapy.

One of his mother's cats, a fat white-and-dark-gray lady, strolled into the living room. Charity smiled and took a few steps away from Arissa's leg to kneel down in front of the animal.

"No, Charity—" she started to say.

"It's okay. Arwen likes kids," Nathan assured her.

Arissa sat on the faded couch, which had been flattened over the years thanks to dog piles of Nathan and his brothers. He sank into his dad's recliner, and his leg bone stopped aching and began to throb instead. "What about the girl at the firefight?" He didn't stutter over the word like he would have a year ago.

"That was Jemma. I didn't know this at the time, but she was rushed to the hospital and had Charity that night. She died a few hours later from complications."

Nathan pressed his lips together. "She was hurt?"

"Scared. Stressed. And she saw her boyfriend die in front of her eyes."

He couldn't look at her. He stood abruptly, ignoring the protest of his leg, and went to close the curtains over the bowfront window. When he had snuck into that garage, he had thought there were only drug dealers and gang members inside. He hadn't known that a young pregnant woman would be there, would be specifically watching Mark, Nathan's partner. She would have seen what Nathan saw—a young Filipino narcotics detective, handing a police case file to one of the drug gang captains.

Selling out his department for an envelope of cash. Mark had been an LAPD mole.

TWO

"What happened to Charity after her parents died?" He spoke quietly so that Charity, distracted by the cat on the other side of the room, wouldn't hear, but Nathan's voice seemed abrupt as he turned from the window to face her again. His green-gray eyes were distant.

Those eyes had once glowed as they looked at her. Now she might as well have disappeared into the floral print on the faded couch she sat on.

"Jemma's parents, the Capunos, took care of Charity until about a year ago. They died in a car pileup on the 101."

A grimace flashed across his mobile mouth at the references to the L.A. freeways. They had once joked about Arissa's terrible sense of direction that often got her lost.

He'd smiled at her, and his eyes had turned to pewter silver, and she had wondered if he felt that magnetic tug between them....

She thrust away the memory and continued, "Jemma's parents apparently never told anyone Charity was Mark's child. When Johnny, Jemma's brother, got custody of her, he found out when he saw Charity's birth certificate. He showed up at my parents' grocery store one day with Charity and said he wouldn't take care of a cop's brat. Then he left Charity there."

Nathan seemed to grow taller, broader, as he stared at her in disbelief. "He just left her? A little girl?"

"Johnny is—"

"I know what he is." A muscle in Nathan's jaw tightened. "I don't have to like his methods."

Johnny's ruthlessness was what had made him rise to become one of the *manoys,* a Captain in the Laki Sa Layaw gang. "It's better this way," she said. "I wouldn't have wanted my niece being raised by a family belonging to the LSL gang, would you?"

His anger at Johnny seemed to fade. "You're right. So your parents took her in?"

Arissa nodded. "I had a paternity test done. She really is Mark's daughter. I just finished the paperwork to become Charity's legal guardian."

"Why not your parents?"

"Dad still isn't comfortable with English and legal documents."

Nathan's brow knit. "His English is fine. I mean, he's a citizen and he's been in the U.S. for, what? Two-thirds of his life?"

"Dad's very proud. He doesn't like doing things imperfectly. His English isn't as good as mine, and he didn't want to make a mistake while going through all the documents."

"So you're Charity's legal guardian. But you're still working for that international airline?"

She nodded. "I'm usually gone for two or three days, and then I have four days off. We have a neighbor who watches Charity with her own kids when my parents have to be at the store."

Nathan shook his head. "I can't believe it. Mark's daughter."

It was a lot to spring on him. He hadn't seen her for over three years—since she'd visited Nathan at the hospital and he'd accused Mark of selling LAPD files and being the reason Nathan was injured.

She swallowed. His words had been so ugly, and he'd been so bitter. But really, what had she expected? All the men she had romantic feelings for had bailed on her whenever her personal life became difficult: her boyfriend dumped her when her mom got cancer, Nathan walked away when Internal Affairs was investigating her brother after his death and the Christian boy she'd been getting close to at church had dramatically backpedaled when Charity entered her life.

She knew better than to count on a man. She wouldn't have come to Nathan for help if she hadn't been desperate. Now she could only hope he would help her, if just for Charity's sake, being Mark's old partner.

"I'm sorry I had to drop in like this," she

said. "I didn't know who else to turn to, and since they mentioned Mark's name…"

"Who?"

She was making a muddle out of all this. *Start at the beginning, Arissa.* "This morning, two Filipino men k-kidnapped me and Charity."

Nathan's face paled, and he stopped pacing to drop back down in the recliner. *"This morning?"*

"I was out with Charity—we were going to get her some new shoes. We had just turned the corner from my parents' grocery store, walking toward my car, when a van pulled up and men jumped out at me. I think they hit me on the back of the head. I woke up in a house still in L.A., not far from my parents' grocery store. I managed to get us out, but before I did, I heard them mention Mark's name. Something about, 'if Mark hadn't died.'"

"It could be any person named Mark—"

"They mentioned it right after saying something about *me,*" Arissa said. "What other Mark could they be talking about?"

"But…" Nathan combed his fingers through his fine, straight brown hair. It was longer than he used to keep it, and it made his eyes seem more shadowed. "Arissa, Mark's been gone for over three years. Why would anyone kidnap you now?"

"That's just it. I don't know. They were speaking Tagalog, not some other Filipino dialect, so I'm thinking they could be from the same area where Mark and I grew up, the same area as my parents' grocery store."

"How did you get away from them?"

She told him. "Then I found my friend Malaya. She has an extra car that used to belong to her aunt, so I asked if I could borrow it. I wasn't sure if the men would come after my parents, so I went home, told them to close up the store, and gave them somewhere to hide."

"Where?"

"I…" This was awkward to mention, especially when they'd had so many arguments about this in the past. "I became a Christian a little over a year ago."

She expected surprise from him, but instead his eyes seemed to grow darker, his mouth tighter. He said nothing, so she continued, "My discipler at church, Mrs. Fuchikami, lives in Pasadena. I knew she'd be willing to help me, so I called her and told her what happened, and asked if she would let my parents stay with her for a little while."

His eyebrows rose. "She said yes?"

"She's very generous." It was a lame way to describe the woman who had been like another mother to her, leading her in a Bible study, showing her and explaining to her the love of Jesus. She would have thought Nathan would be happy for her, but instead he seemed grim. Had what happened to him affected his faith, too? "After I took them to Mrs. Fuchikami's house, I drove here with Charity." It had been a relatively smooth eight hours of driving, but she'd been tense the entire way, desperately trying to be cheerful for Charity's sake, but scared to the core.

Nathan was shaking his head. "You should have gone to the police, Arissa."

"What could they have done? We both

know that area—the gangs rule those streets. If this is related to the drug gang that killed Mark, what hope do I have that the police can protect us? And my parents?"

Pain flashed across Nathan's face, and he abruptly stood again. This time he went to lean against the quaint fireplace mantel. "What in the world did Mark *do,* Arissa?"

Her jaw clenched. "He didn't do *anything.*" Three years ago, the Internal Affairs investigation had turned up nothing and his name had been cleared of Nathan's accusation.

Nathan turned to look at her, his eyes burning. "Arissa, I saw him in that chop shop."

"Isn't there a chance you misunderstood what you saw?"

"No," he ground out.

"I saw the police report. There wasn't any proof—"

"There also wasn't a good explanation for why he was even there."

He was right. And Mark had been a narcotics detective, so he had no business entering a building smack-dab in the middle of LSL territory. "It might have had nothing to do with the police. Maybe that's why his girlfriend was there."

Nathan stilled, like a statue of cold marble. She'd finally pricked his anger.

She'd mulled over that day and that police report dozens of times, but until a few months ago, she hadn't known about Charity's mother, a sister to one of the gang leaders. Before, she hadn't wanted to believe Nathan's accusation about Mark just because of her loyalty to her brother, but now she was convinced there was another explanation for why Mark had been there.

She waited to feel the anger at what he'd done in reporting Mark's actions in the chop shop to Internal Affairs, in causing so much stress for her family as IA made such horrible insinuations and investigated her brother. She waited to feel the triumph that he'd been wrong, that Internal Affairs had cleared Mark's name.

But all she felt was the old longing, a familiar bittersweet stirring in her chest. Nathan had once meant so much to her, had caused such a rush of excitement every time she happened to see him, which seemed more often than mere chance. She remembered the anxiety and hope as she wondered if he felt the same way about her. Seeing him now brought back old memories of happier times rather than the hurt and betrayal she'd felt in the months after Mark's death.

Nathan's face hardened again, and he gave a short shake of his head. "I can't talk about this, Arissa." He shifted his weight, and a wince of pain flashed across his face.

She swallowed, remembering that day in the hospital, what he'd shouted to her about his shattered leg. About how he would never walk again because of Mark. The words still cut.

She took a deep breath and straightened her spine. Seeing him again had caught her up in too many memories. What was past should stay there. She hoped Nathan would help her, but she couldn't fool herself into thinking their relationship would ever be anything remotely like it had once been.

And what had it been? Just good friends. *No,* an insidious voice said inside of her.

You saw the way he looked at you. Spoke to you. Touched you. You were becoming deeper than friends, even if he hadn't definitely said anything to you, even if he hadn't yet kissed you.

Her cheeks warmed, and she turned her attention to where Charity chatted to Arwen the cat, who was sprawled across the little girl's lap and purring very loudly as Charity stroked the soft fur. Charity was her priority now, not any misty "maybes" from the past.

"Aside from your parents and your friend, does anyone else know you're here in Sonoma?" Nathan asked.

She shook her head. "They don't know where we are. I tried to be careful."

He sighed. "So you were kidnapped this morning, but you don't know who did it except that they mentioned the name Mark. You're not giving me a lot to go on, Arissa."

"You still think I should go to the police with this wealth of information?"

He ignored her sarcasm. "Do you have your cell phone?"

"No, I dumped it. I told my parents to

dump theirs, too. I know it's easy to have those traced these days, even if you're not in law enforcement."

The look he gave her seemed bitter. "Did Mark teach you that?"

His tone got her back up. "No, actually, my neighbor's youngest boy wanted to teach me how to boost cars, and he's the one who told me."

He frowned at her. "Why would a flight attendant need to know how to steal a car?" he demanded.

"I'll tell you if you'll stop treating me like a criminal," she fired back.

He looked away. "Sorry," he mumbled.

"I don't know what to do next, how to keep us both safe." She glanced at Charity and noticed that the humidity had turned her silken hair into a nest of loose flyaway curls. Maybe this had been a mistake. She wasn't sure Nathan would help her, even if he could. She had thought that since Internal Affairs hadn't found any proof against Mark, Nathan's attitude would have changed, but apparently not.

Nathan rubbed his forehead with his palm, a gesture she remembered from when he was thinking through a problem.

"First we need to cover your tracks," he finally said. "We can think about your other options tomorrow when I'm not so tired."

He was going to help them. Arissa fought an absurd urge to cry.

"You and Charity can stay in the guest bedroom."

"Thanks," she said.

"Where did you park your friend's car?"

"On the street about two houses down."

"Let's drive it into the garage behind the house." He headed toward the front door. "That way it'll be out on the street for as little time as possible. No one can happen to remember seeing it or recall a partial license plate."

Nathan was ever the cop.

She left Charity dozing with the cat and followed him outside. As they approached Malaya's car, they suddenly saw a faint bluish light flash from the backseat.

Nathan grabbed her, and his nearness sent

a whiff of musk and lime curling around her. Her heart sped up. It must be from the unexpected light from the car.

He approached the car so quietly that all she heard was the crickets from the neighbor's bushes. He peered inside, and another blue light flashed, illuminating the perplexed look on his face.

Then suddenly he was scrabbling at the rear door handle, but it was locked.

She handed him the car keys. "What is it?"

He opened the door, diving into the backseat, and emerged with a cell phone, which had just received a text message: M where R U?

Oh, no. "That's Malaya's."

"It was just visible under the passenger seat." Nathan's face was grim. "Does anyone know you borrowed her car? Her family or friends?"

"No, she and I were alone."

"None of her neighbors saw her?"

She bit her lip. "I didn't see them…"

"If the gang finds out you took Malaya's car, they might think to try to track her cell phone. And it's been on the entire drive up to Sonoma, plus the whole time we were talking."

"Would they really figure it out that fast?"

"You escaped. That means they still need to kidnap you, but they've lost the element of surprise. They'll be following every connection to you that they can think of."

She made to turn off the phone but he stopped her. "They might think you only stopped in Sonoma for gas and food. Let's use this cell phone to our advantage. We have to take the phone and the car north, tonight."

"With Charity?"

"I can call my parents and ask them to cut their dinner short to come home to watch her."

She cringed at the thought of leaving Charity. She already thought of her niece as if she were her own daughter. Besides, Charity had been very clingy since they'd escaped. The cat had been the only thing to get her to let Arissa go. It seemed very unlikely that Charity would let her aunt leave her behind. "No, don't do that. Besides, Charity's car seat is already in Malaya's car."

As they hurried back to the house, Nathan checked his watch. "Let me make a phone call before we go."

"Who?"

"My friend in LAPD narcotics."

"What for?" she demanded.

"Calm down, I'm just following a hunch." He got out his cell phone and dialed.

She did calm down, because Mark had always trusted Nathan's hunches. She entered the house just as Nathan started speaking into his phone.

"Steve, it's Nathan Fischer. I had a question about the LSL gang. Call me back when you get the chance." He hung up the phone.

"I know the LSLs were at the chop shop when Mark died, but I don't understand why they're after me, and especially after all these years."

"I don't know. Other Filipino gangs speak Tagalog." He shrugged and shook his head. "It's just a hunch."

Mark had always said Nathan did two

things extremely well—he was an expert shot with a handgun, and his gut instinct was usually dead on. Both those things also usually got them in a heap of trouble, Mark had said with a laugh.

And now, she had no one else she could turn to, no one else who might be able to figure out why those men had kidnapped her, and what the connection was to Mark. But did her presence only bring up bad memories of the day his best friend died and his career ended? And could she really trust those instincts when they led him to accuse her brother?

She was beautiful in her sleep.

Nathan couldn't stop himself from glancing over at Arissa in the passenger seat of Malaya's car. This particular stretch of freeway was lined with lights, spaced widely apart. Every time they passed under a pool of white, he would look over and see her face, relaxed in sleep, vulnerable. No sign of her stress, her worry, the jumpiness that had dogged her all the way from L.A. She leaned her head against the closed window, exposing the graceful column of her throat.

Before her mom's cancer—was it five years ago?—she'd been a party girl, lively and bubbly. Nathan had been attracted to her for a long time, but she was a bit wild *and* his partner's sister, which made her off limits.

And, at the time, the fact she wasn't a Christian had mattered to him. He snorted in bitter irony at how the tables were turned. He'd given up on God just when she started believing in Him.

But despite her social lifestyle, when her family needed her, she had been there one hundred percent, according to what Mark had told Nathan. There was no trace of the party girl anymore. And now, she looked like…a mother.

He glanced in the rearview mirror at Charity, asleep in her car seat. Poor kid had had an exhausting day, too.

The sight of her brought back all the memories he'd tried to bury.

He had originally snuck into that LSL gang

chop shop because he'd seen Mark enter the place. Back at the station, he had noticed his partner furtively slip a case folder into his jacket before heading out the door. The Gangs and Narcotics Division had had several drug raids happen too late, the occupants of the drug houses long gone by the time they got there, and Nathan suspected a mole. So when he saw Mark's unusual actions, he was suspicious, even though he didn't want to be. He hadn't wanted to believe that his friend and partner was betraying his fellow cops.

But he followed Mark to that LSL chop shop, crouched behind a barrel and saw Mark hand the case folder to Johnny Capuno. Johnny was about to hand Mark a bulging envelope when there was a shout behind Nathan and bullets started flying.

Johnny pocketed the envelope and the case folder and escaped, which was why Internal Affairs never found any evidence on Mark's body that he was a mole.

That day, Mark hid behind a Lexus. Other gang members peppered Nathan's shield, a

Buick, with gunfire. Nathan returned fire and shot one of them, then ran behind a Trans Am.

Then Mark pointed his gun straight at Nathan.

Nathan's heart stopped as if the bullet had already plunged deep. But then Mark *missed*.

Nathan brought his gun up...but didn't fire.

The next thing he had known, his leg felt like it had been blown apart. Just the memory made his hands shake against the steering wheel.

He had reluctantly told Internal Affairs about seeing Mark give Johnny the case folder. He knew if Mark was found to have sold information to the LSL gang, Mark's family wouldn't receive his pension. The Tiongs desperately needed the money after Mrs. Tiong's surgery a couple years before Mark's death. But IA hadn't found any proof and the investigation was dropped.

He'd never told the Tiongs about seeing Mark take aim at him. It was bad enough they'd had to endure the questions from Internal Affairs after Mark's funeral. So he'd kept his secret, but it pained him to hear from Arissa's lips how she believed her brother was innocent.

Nathan couldn't deny what he'd seen before the gunfight. Mark's actions hadn't been those of an innocent man. And now, Mark was gone.

Nathan missed him. And not just him.

Except for that one angry conversation with Arissa, he hadn't seen any of the Tiong family in over three years. Until tonight. If this was the LSL gang, why would they be after Arissa *now,* so long after the fact?

An insidious thought twisted its way into his head, a thought he'd been trying to keep at bay. Arissa and Mark had grown up on the same streets as the LSL gang members, knew them from their childhood. Why would the gang be after her if she didn't know anything? Was she really as innocent as he'd like to believe her to be? He didn't want to think it of her, but he also hadn't wanted to believe Mark would betray his badge.

Except that Nathan had once known Arissa

well. She was fiercely loyal to her family, and fiercely protective. If she did know something that would put her in danger, she would have done everything she could to protect Charity and her parents. She wouldn't have left herself and a three-year-old child open to attack that way.

The LSLs were known to be part of a drug cartel that consisted of four Filipino gangs. Why did they kidnap her as opposed to simply killing her? What did they need from her?

Arissa awoke with a start and a sharply indrawn breath. She blinked at her surroundings, then at him. For a moment, her eyes seemed to light up with an expression he hadn't seen in three years. Then they turned to look out the car windows, and her face became grave again. "How long until we reach the truck stop?"

"Another hour."

"The cell phone won't die before we get there, will it?"

He glanced down to where he'd propped it in the open ashtray. He pressed a button to look at the amount of charge left in it. "It think it'll have plenty of juice by the time we get to the stop. When you leave it in the women's restroom, don't leave it in the open. Put it someplace a little out of the way so no stranger will find it immediately and try to contact Malaya about her phone."

"Or someone might just take her phone," Arissa commented. "It's one of the latest models."

"I hope they don't. If they have it while the men after you are tracking it…" He didn't want any more innocents suffering in all this.

"Let me try to get hold of her again." Arissa picked up a new prepaid cell phone they'd bought at a gas station a few miles back and tried calling Malaya's home phone number. "Still no answer. I left a message on the answering machine at her parents' house, too, but before I left L.A., she mentioned that they're out of town this week."

A green rest stop sign flashed as they passed it. "Can we stop?" she asked. "I need to use the restroom."

He turned into the rest stop. The outdoor floodlights cast a sickly yellow glow over the parking spaces directly in front of the low buildings. Despite the late hour, there was a scattering of cars and a couple big rigs. Weary travelers making a pit stop wandered around the two main buildings and the kiosks with drink and snack machines.

Nathan walked around near the parked car, stretching his legs, easing the cramp in his injured thigh. He kept an eye on Charity, still sound asleep in the back of the car.

A black BMW SUV pulled into the rest stop, its bright headlights dispelling the gloom for a moment before it parked a few spaces down from them. Two men got out and headed toward Nathan on their way to the restrooms.

Except they didn't walk like travelers who needed to use the bathrooms. They walked like predators stalking a kill—their eyes swept the area around the buildings, pausing briefly on a tall slim woman buying a soda at one of the vending machines, again on a shorter woman walking her dog in the grassy area. They strode purposely, quickly.

Nathan found himself immediately slipping into his narcotics detective role once again. He remained nonchalant, maintaining his cover as a motorist just stretching his legs, but he cast furtive glances at the two men.

As they passed him, he clearly saw their faces.

It took all his strength not to start in surprise.

THREE

LSL gang members. Nathan remembered their faces from his years in narcotics. He even recalled one of them as a flashing glimpse of a scared face as the man fled from the chop shop during the firefight.

The men looked directly at him and then casually looked away. They didn't recognize him at all. But they would recognize Arissa. He knew in his gut that's who they were looking for.

He followed them, and one of them answered his cell phone. "Yeah, we're here... No, we don't see her yet."

At that moment, Arissa walked out of the women's restroom and headed toward Nathan.

The backs of the two men stiffened. They reached into their jackets.

Nathan had his Glock out in a split second. "Freeze! Police!"

The two men whirled around, guns raised, and Nathan darted behind a circular bulletin kiosk as the first shots were fired. The few bystanders scattered. Thank goodness there weren't many people who might be hit by a stray bullet or a ricochet.

He peered around the other side of the kiosk, saw Arissa dashing for the car. He had to get there, too, so they could drive away. He fired a few return shots, and the two men took cover behind a huge metal recycling receptacle. Now was his chance. He aimed three shots in their direction, then sprinted for the car.

But his leg wouldn't hold him. After being stationary for a couple hours, a few scant minutes of stretching weren't enough and his leg buckled under him in a bloom of pain. He landed on the asphalt of the walkway, gravel biting into his palm and prickling his jaw.

He couldn't even run for his life!

But Arissa could. She sprinted toward the

car and dove into the passenger side, then slithered to the driver's seat. The engine fired up as Nathan hoisted himself to his feet and took cover behind an oak tree. A bullet rained splinters on his shoulder.

"Go!" he told her. "Get out of here!" He wasn't sure if she could hear him. He fired at the two men.

There was a sudden screech and thump as Arissa drove the car up onto the curb, across the grass and the walkway, to jerk to a stop next to the tree. A bullet pinged off the frame and she screamed, "Get in!" even as she leaned over to open the passenger-side door. The sound of Charity's crying rang in counterpoint to the bullets whizzing past.

He dove in, yanking the door closed behind him. "Go! Go!"

She took off with tires throwing up clods of grass and dirt. Cranking on the wheel, she bounced back into the parking lot, but she hadn't turned on the headlights and narrowly missed hitting a parked car.

She flipped on the headlights. "How do

I get out of here?" She flinched as a bullet shattered a tail light.

"Just get us away from them!" Nathan rolled down the window and fired at the two men, who were running after them into the parking lot. When Nathan fired, they ducked behind their car.

The old car's headlights were feeble and narrow, and Arissa swerved around a bush before jamming down a straight stretch of the parking lot. Nathan didn't recognize this part of the rest stop. They entered a small side ramp and drove under the freeway.

"Where are we going?"

"I don't know!" Arissa said.

The small street emptied them into another parking lot, similar to the one they'd just left. "This is the other rest area on the opposite side of the freeway," Nathan said.

"I'm not going back toward two men shooting at us." Arissa found the freeway exit. She jammed the car onto the on-ramp and suddenly they were back on the freeway—but going in the opposite direction, heading south and not north.

The only sound in the car now was Charity's crying. "It's all right, *nene.*" Arissa tried to soothe her with glances in the rearview mirror. "Don't be frightened. We're okay now."

"At the next exit, get off and we'll switch," Nathan said. "I'll turn us around and heard north again for a little while in case they're following us."

Arissa nodded.

"I recognized them," Nathan said. "They're LSLs."

She was silent for a moment. "I guess that answers that question. But there are still the questions of why they want me—and why now?"

"Where's Malaya's cell phone?"

"There was nowhere to hide it in the restroom so I tossed it out of the car back in the rest area parking lot. I can't think of any other way they could have tracked us so soon."

Nathan couldn't, either. But what concerned him more was the fact the LSL gang had managed to run a trace on the cell phone so quickly in the first place. It could be done with private companies, but not this fast. No, the only ones who could do it this quickly were law enforcement.

Did the LSL gang have another mole in the LAPD?

They rode in silence, punctuated only by Arissa's soothing remarks to Charity and the girl's hiccuping cries that slowly died down as she drifted back to sleep.

As Arissa got off at the next exit ramp, Nathan's cell phone rang. His stomach lurched as Steve Thompson's name appeared on caller ID. Did Steve have something to do with the attack tonight? He felt ugly thinking about it. Steve had been a friend for years. In fact, he had helped Nathan a few months ago when Nathan's friend, Shaun O'Neill, had needed information.

But the LSL gang had managed to somehow track Arissa to that rest stop. When they'd been speaking on the phone with someone, they had known Arissa was there. What if Steve was the mole? Should Nathan lie and pretend they hadn't just gotten shot at? Or should Nathan at least act as if he trusted Steve?

Steve. His friend. Just like Mark had been his best friend and partner, the man he'd trusted his life to day after day. Were they both moles after all? The betrayal bit deep in his stomach.

He answered the phone on the last ring. "Hey, Steve."

"Hey, buddy, what's up? Haven't heard from you in a few months. You out of physical therapy by now? How's everything going?" Steve's usual cheerful chitchat, nothing out of the ordinary. No pumping Nathan for information or trying to figure out what Nathan might know or not know.

"Uh..."

Steve's voice deepened. "Uh-oh. What's wrong? Your voice mail message only said you had a question about the LSLs. Please tell me you're not in trouble with them."

"Steve, what have you heard about them lately?"

A slight pause. Then shuffling, a bit of bumping, and when Steve spoke again, his voice was quieter and slightly muffled. "Look, I'm not talking to you, okay? That information is classified, so I'm not telling you about how there's word on the street that the LSLs are looking for someone, but they won't say who or why. And I'm definitely never going to speak about how all this activity only started about a week ago."

"Who are they looking for?"

"Most of the snitches I've talked to lately don't even know if it's a man or a woman. But they all say that the LSLs are *stressed*. And you and I both know that stressed drug lords make unhappy campers." A pause, then, "Hey, they're not after *you,* are they? Please tell me no. Fischer, even you can't be that dumb."

"They're not after me." But had those two men gotten a good look at Nathan's face in the dim parking lot? They hadn't recognized him, but would they be able to describe him to someone who would? After all, he had been Mark's partner, and Mark had been their mole.

And Steve might be a mole, too, but Nathan needed to pretend he didn't suspect him. He closed his eyes and gritted his teeth. He didn't want to think this way about his friend, but he couldn't be stupid, either. What to tell him? So far, no one knew Arissa had come to him for help. If Steve was a mole, Nathan needed to dissuade him from making the connection.

"I called you because I'm driving Mom to Sacramento for a few days," Nathan told Steve. "I stopped in this rest stop and thought I recognized an LSL gang member, but it's been three years, so I wasn't sure. I wanted to know if there were any rumblings about the LSLs moving north." He gave a short laugh. "That sounds like I'm trying to tell you how to do your job. Sorry, I can't seem to stop being a cop."

Steve chuckled, too. "Buddy, you're starting to be like those retired guys who call me every so often to ask about current cases."

"Hey, I'm not that old yet." He tried to sound jovial.

"Anyway, no, I haven't heard anything about the LSLs moving north, although

I don't deal too much with the Filipino gangs—the Hispanic gangs keep me busy enough. Which LSL did you think you saw?"

"I don't remember his name. I thought I saw him at the chop shop." He didn't have to elaborate. Steve had been one of the officers on the scene, finding Nathan bleeding near the car he had hidden behind.

"Yeah, I would think those guys would be imprinted on your memory." Steve's voice was uncharacteristically grim. "Well, is there anything else I can *not* tell you about the LSLs?"

"No. Now I feel kinda stupid for even calling you. Sorry, Steve."

"Hey, no problem, buddy. Next time you're in L.A., call me. It's been too long."

"I know it has. I'll keep in touch." It occurred to Nathan that if Steve was a mole, it might be wise to keep his "enemies" close.

When they returned to Sonoma, there was still a light on in the living room of the Fischers' home. "Do your parents usually leave the living room lights on?" Arissa asked Nathan.

"No." He steered the car down the narrow driveway that ran alongside the house to park next to the garage in the back of the property. "They must be waiting up for us."

While driving back to Sonoma, he had received a phone call that seemed to be from his mom. Nathan explained that Arissa and Charity had come and asked if they could stay at the house for a few days.

"You're sure your mom said it was all right?" Arissa unbuckled Charity from her car seat and hoisted the sleeping girl onto her shoulder. "I mean, she's never met me."

"It's fine, really. Here, let me take her." Nathan walked around the car and took Charity from her arms.

He was very close, and it was almost as if the night cloaked them, wrapping around them in its velvet folds. She smelled musk and lime again, mingled with the gardenias growing at the back of the house. Her skin tingled as he stared down at her for a long moment.

Then the back porch light flickered on, and Arissa blinked at the sudden brightness. The back door unlocked and swung inward, then a smiling woman with silver-blond curls pushed open the screen door. "You must be Arissa. And that's Charity?"

"Hi, Mrs. Fischer." Arissa headed toward the back door with her heart pounding. She tried to keep her voice light, but was afraid it sounded a bit breathless.

"Call me Kat," Nathan's mom said. "Or Mama Kat. That's what your brother called me."

Nathan had been following Arissa into the house, but he paused for a moment. "He did? I don't remember that."

Kat blinked at Nathan as if thinking about something, then said, "No, I guess you wouldn't know that, since you weren't here."

Nathan's perplexed eyes found Arissa's as they stepped into the kitchen. Then he looked at his mother. "Mom, what are you talking about?"

"Mark called me Mama Kat when he came to dinner."

Nathan froze in his tracks. "Wait…Mom, *Mark Tiong* came to visit you in *Sonoma?*" His brow creased, and the corners of his eyes tightened.

"You mean, without Nathan?" Arissa asked his mom.

"Oh, yes." Kat led the way toward the bedrooms. "Let's put down that sleeping girl and we can talk in the living room."

Kat chatted about nothing in particular as Arissa took off Charity's shoes and clothes and pulled on her nightgown, but this news about Mark kept distracting her. He and Nathan had been good friends, beyond just being partners, and she knew Mark had gone to Sonoma with Nathan and met his parents several times. But she hadn't known Mark had been so close to the Fischers that he'd come up to Sonoma without Nathan. And why wouldn't he have told Nathan about it?

Kat closed the bedroom door. "Now let me brew you some mint tea."

"Oh, no, that's—" Arissa started to say, but Kat waved her off.

"No, it's no trouble." Kat bustled back toward the kitchen.

Nathan, who had been waiting outside the bedroom door, gave Arissa a helpless shrug. "Come meet my dad."

Mr. Fischer put away the newspaper he was reading and rose from the recliner as they entered the living room. "Nice to meet you. Call me Robert."

As she shook his hand, Arissa noticed that Nathan had gotten his solid physical build and his fine, straight brown hair from his father, although Robert's was streaked with gray.

Nathan sank onto the couch, and since the worn rocking chair looked like it belonged to Kat, Arissa sat down next to him. She could feel the heat from his body even though several inches lay between them. He stretched his arm across the back of the couch, and although he didn't touch her, she could almost feel the warmth of his skin against her neck.

Kat came in with a tray and four steaming mugs of tea, each mug a different style.

Arissa picked up the red Japanese-style mug and sipped the strong tea.

Nathan picked the blue Norwegian mug but didn't drink from it. He immediately said, "Mom, when did Mark come to visit you guys?"

Kat took her time, sipping from her delicate English teacup before answering. "We saw him a few times around downtown in the year before he died. I'm sorry, dear," she said to Arissa. "It doesn't pain you to talk about him, does it?"

"No." She hadn't known he'd gone to Sonoma. Then again, he could make the trip in a day, driving up and spending a few hours, then driving back to L.A. in the evening.

"Mom, you never told me this," Nathan said.

"I didn't really think it was anything unusual. He joined us for dinner several times with you, so when we saw him by himself a couple times, we invited him for dinner."

Robert nodded. "It was only once or twice he had dinner with us."

Kat leaned forward, her green eyes gleaming. "I thought at first he had a girlfriend up in Sonoma whom he was visiting, but then he mentioned he was visiting an aunt here."

"Oh." Arissa relaxed. "Yes, she married my mom's brother, although my uncle died when I was a kid."

"After Mark died," Kat said to Nathan, "I thought it might be too painful for you to talk about him."

Nathan's eyes fell. "Yeah, Mom, I can understand that."

"You want to tell us why you're here?" Robert asked bluntly but kindly.

"Robert," Kat admonished him.

"No, you deserve to know." Arissa explained everything—the kidnapping, the cell phone, the attack at the rest stop.

"Gracious." Kat's eyes were wide. "Thank the Lord you're all right, and Charity, too."

At his mother's words, Nathan's eyes slid away. That was the second time references to God made him uncomfortable. What had happened to him? He had been a strong Christian when she'd known him down south. Had his faith changed so much in the past three years?

Well, he'd lost his career, a job he did very well. He'd lost his best friend. His leg obviously still pained him, years later, so he'd lost his athleticism, too. Maybe all that turned him away from God?

Robert frowned as he sipped his cooled tea. "How did the LSL gang members know you had your friend's car and cell phone?"

Arissa shook her head. "I have no idea. Maybe someone saw me driving out of L.A. in Malaya's car. Since I had gotten rid of my cell phone, they could have thought to trace hers, thinking she was with me."

They might go after Malaya, if they believed she knew where Arissa was. She had to get in touch with her friend.

Robert asked his son, "Is it possible for them to trace the cell phone so quickly? I thought only cops can do that."

Nathan nodded slowly.

A chill ran down her arms, and she sipped her tea. "Those men were right on my tail. After I escaped, I went straight to Malaya's house. I went home to pack a bag and get my folks to leave, but I was there for less than an hour before I dropped my parents off with a friend and then headed north. And I was here in Sonoma for only an hour before we went north again. We've been on the move constantly except for those two hours, but they still caught up to us at that rest stop."

Nathan's eyes were intent as he looked at her. "I think the LSL gang managed to have someone in the LAPD trace the phone for them."

"You didn't tell your LAPD friend, right?" Arissa said. "I heard you call him."

"I didn't tell him anything."

But there might be someone in LAPD who was being paid by the LSLs. She shivered, wondering what would have happened to her and Charity if she'd gone to the police as soon as she had escaped.

"Did those gang members get a good look at you at the rest stop?" Robert asked Nathan.

His mouth was grim. "I'm not sure. It was light enough that I could recognize that one guy from the chop shop, so they may have seen me well enough to remember me later or describe me to someone."

Startled, Arissa glanced at Robert and Kat. "If they figure out you're Mark's partner, they can look up your family's address here in Sonoma." She'd put his parents in danger, too.

First Malaya, now the Fischers. *She* had done this. She had to fix it. She didn't know how, and the stress was a weight across her shoulders.

"We have some time." It was obvious Nathan was trying to soothe her. "Let me talk to someone about helping you and Charity disappear."

"And my parents," Arissa insisted. "They have to know if they had my parents, I'd do anything."

"And your parents," Nathan agreed.

Kat reached forward and took her hand. "Don't blame yourself. None of this is your fault. Everything will be fine—just trust in the Lord."

The words felt cold and empty. She and Charity were so alone.

Robert's blue-gray eyes caught hers. "Something else you should consider. If you want to protect yourself, you need to know why they're after you."

"But I *don't* know why they're after me."

"They kidnapped you rather than simply killing you," Nathan said. "Maybe Mark had something they need."

"Like what?" She tensed, not wanting to hear him bring up his accusations again. But after seeing the LSLs at the rest stop, the horrible suspicion began to sprout like a thorn.

Nathan's mouth tightened for a moment. "Maybe he…stumbled across something. And even though your aunt is here and Mom's roast beef is awesome—" he smiled at Kat "—I don't think that's the only reason why he was in Sonoma those few times in the months before his death."

"That still doesn't explain why they tried to kidnap me *now*. He's been gone for over three years."

"Maybe they only recently discovered Mark had...whatever it is he had," Kat said.

"And they figure you have it now," Nathan said, "or at least know about it."

Arissa shook her head. "I don't know anything. He never talked about his work with us. He was very conscientious."

"He didn't seem stressed or secretive the months before he died?" There was a hardness and focus in Nathan's eyes, as if he wanted to siphon the information out of her like drawing blood.

"Nothing like that." That's why she couldn't believe he was a mole. He hadn't acted differently at all in the times she'd been home from a flight and hung out with him.

"Maybe he just kept it from you," Kat said.

"It's hard to keep anything from your family when you're all living in the same two-bedroom apartment," Arissa said drily.

Nathan's head cocked. "I knew Mark lived with your folks, but you were living there, too? I thought you had your own apartment in L.A."

She shook her head. "When Mom got the

cancer diagnosis and the medical bills started coming in, Mark and I decided to let go of our apartments and live with our folks. The money we used to spend on rent we gave to Dad to help pay for the bills."

"You can hide anything if you're determined enough," Robert said. "We had three boys in this small house and they managed to hide plenty from each other."

"You should go look through Mark's things," Kat said.

"There isn't anything," Arissa said. "Internal Affairs already—"

She shut her mouth and counted her heartbeats in the silence. Kat looked down at her teacup. Robert frowned out the window. Only Nathan looked at her, but his eyes seemed sad this time, rather than angry.

Finally he spoke, and his voice was soft. "Maybe there was something innocent-looking that wouldn't mean anything to a stranger, but would seem odd to someone who knew Mark well."

"But what?"

"Maybe it's something small that would

lead to what the gang wants. An address, or a phone number."

She squeezed her eyes shut and rubbed her temples with her fingers. If Mark had something the LSLs wanted—or even if they thought he had something they wanted—didn't that point to the fact he might have been a mole? For so long, she'd been denying that it could be possible, especially in light of the lack of evidence, but maybe that evidence had been hidden in plain sight in the midst of Mark's things left behind.

Her brother, an LAPD mole. It was too horrible.

But she had to face the possibility now, because Charity's life was in danger. "Mark's things are down in L.A."

"Then you should get to bed," Robert said. "You have a road trip tomorrow."

It was the obvious move for them. She needed to figure out what the gang wanted from her unless she preferred to be on the run for the rest of her life, putting people she loved in danger.

FOUR

Even as Nathan hefted his mother's suitcase into the trunk of their car, she followed to repeat, "I still don't understand why we need to go into hiding. I think you're being a little paranoid."

Nathan drew in a breath to answer her yet again when his father appeared with his suitcase. "Kat, let it go."

She gave a little pout but said nothing.

"Mom, I wouldn't tell you to do something so drastic if I didn't think it was necessary."

"But even you said that the gang members didn't recognize you when they looked straight at you at the rest stop," his mom said. "And then after the shooting started, would they really have gotten a better look?"

"Even if they didn't know me, they might have seen enough of me to describe me, and other gang members might remember I was Mark's partner." Nathan put his father's suitcase in the car and shut the trunk.

Arissa appeared, holding Charity in her arms. "I'm sorry for inconveniencing you like this. If I had realized I'd be putting you in danger, I wouldn't have come here. I'd have found some other way to talk to Nathan."

"It wouldn't have mattered because as soon as the gang knows I'm helping you, it's too easy to look up my parents' address." Nathan turned to his father. "You have everything you need?"

He nodded and fumbled in his back pocket, producing the burner cell phone Nathan had given to him that morning. "I have this, too."

"Don't use it unless you need to."

At that moment, a police cruiser turned the corner at the end of the street and approached them. When it parked, Detective Carter and two uniformed officers got out of the car.

Arissa swallowed and sidled closer to him. "What are they here for?"

"I asked Detective Carter to help us out. I'd trust him with my life."

The wariness in her eyes eased, and she nodded.

The gesture made the tension in his gut ease, and yet at the same time he wanted to distance himself from her, so he walked toward the detective.

"Nathan, these are the two officers who'll be watching your parents' house." Detective Carter gestured to the two men with him. "Charlie Granger and Joseph Fong."

Nathan smiled. "Charlie, good to see you. It's been a while." He shook hands with the sandy-haired young man.

"You know each other?" Detective Carter asked.

Charlie grinned, his dimples making him look younger than his twenty-something age. "My family and the Fischers go to the same church. Nathan was my mentor for almost five years when I was high school."

"Only during the summers, when I was home from college." Charlie hadn't lost the charm that gave all the girls crushes on him.

"How long have you been in the Sonoma police department?"

"Well, I was an accountant for a few years, but then I decided to switch to law enforcement a few years ago."

Nathan turned to the other officer and shook his hand. He was a few years younger than Charlie. "Pleased to meet you. Are you new to Sonoma?"

The Chinese man nodded. "I moved a few months ago."

"Did you transfer from another city?"

Joseph smiled. "Los Angeles, actually."

Nathan couldn't suppress his surprise. "Where?"

"Atwater Village."

"I was in Glassell Park."

Joseph's eyebrows rose. "We were near neighbors. I was there for two years, then moved up here to Sonoma."

So he was in Atwater during the time Nathan had been recovering in Sonoma. "Why'd you move here?"

Joseph's eyes slid away for a moment, then

back to him. "Needed a change of pace." His voice had a more clipped quality than before.

Was Nathan being paranoid? He shook it off. "How do you like it here?"

"Less gunshots." Joseph chuckled.

Detective Carter and Charlie greeted Nathan's parents as they approached with Arissa, and he heard the young officer ask, "Where will you be going, Mrs. Fischer?"

Nathan immediately turned toward them, but his mom caught his eye and said, "Sorry, Charlie, but Nathan said I shouldn't say."

"Oh, I totally understand." Charlie nodded.

Detective Carter glanced at Nathan, his expression neutral, not giving away that he already knew their destination. "Officer Granger and Officer Fong will be the ones keeping a watch over the house for you," he explained to Mr. and Mrs. Fischer.

"Why do you need to watch the house?" Arissa asked.

"In case the gang members figure out it was me with you at the rest stop," Nathan said. "If they come here snooping, I wanted someone on the watch for them."

His father nodded. "Wise of you."

Nathan turned to the two officers. "I appreciate you doing this for me."

Joseph nodded, but the gaze he turned to Arissa seemed a bit speculative. What was the man thinking at that moment?

Nathan shook off the thought as Charlie said, "The only thing missing will be your corned beef, Mrs. Fischer."

She laughed and gave him a playful swat on the arm.

Detective Carter shook Nathan's hand again, his gray eyes searching his face. "You'll be all right?"

"We'll be fine."

"If we see any strangers around your house, I'll call you right away." The detective was doing Nathan a huge favor in setting two of his officers to watch the house, but the threat of gang members in Sonoma was enough to put him on alert.

"It'll only be for a few days. If they haven't shown up by then, it's likely they couldn't identify me."

The officers left, including Charlie, who

said he'd be back in plain clothes in a few minutes to keep an eye on the house.

Nathan kissed his mother on the cheek. "Have fun."

"We'll try." They were going to stay at a retired detective's home in Napa, a friend of Detective Carter's. It was near some hiking trails they would enjoy. They'd used to go as a family until Nathan's accident—he couldn't last on the trails anymore with his bum leg.

Acid rose up to burn Nathan's throat. He swallowed and said brusquely to Arissa, "Are you ready to go?"

She seemed taken aback by his tone, but nodded and went to strap Charity into the car seat in the back of his SUV.

Nathan's father regarded him with a look that was half stern, half questioning. His mother's eyebrows rose, but all she said was, "Take care of them." However, her delivery was the same as if she'd said, *Be nice.*

As they all got into their cars, Nathan admitted that a part of him didn't want to be nice—a part of him wanted to push Arissa away. Because this woman, more than any other, had gotten under his skin, and he couldn't allow that to happen again.

His leg had given out at the rest stop. Who knew what else might happen. What if his body kept letting them down? He was only half a man, now, and he couldn't afford for anyone to get close to him.

Especially not this woman and child. They needed someone they could count on—not a man who would fail them just when they needed him most.

Arissa's breath caught as she saw the mangled lock on her parents' apartment door. The wood of the door had long, jagged cracks and splinters littered the floor.

Suddenly Nathan shoved her behind him, and his gun appeared in his hands. He approached the door, ajar a crack, and listened.

Arissa knelt beside Charity, her arms around the girl. "Shh, keep quiet, *nene,*" she whispered. Charity picked up on her tension and wrapped soft arms around Arissa's neck, burying her head in her hair.

Nathan eased open the door silently and slowly entered the apartment. Arissa remained in the landing, gripping Charity with shaking hands.

She shouldn't be surprised. Someone had been after her, so naturally they'd search her apartment. More than ever she was grateful she'd thought to make her parents close the grocery store and stay with her discipler from church. The gangs would never find Mrs. Fuchikami—she had never visited Arissa, and the only connection to her would be Arissa's cell phone. When she'd escaped and returned to her parents' grocery store, they had told her they'd found her purse and cell phone on the street when she didn't return with Charity in one hour as expected. Arissa had promptly destroyed the cell phone and the SIM card with the phone numbers on it.

It seemed like hours but it must have been only minutes before Nathan appeared again in the doorway and motioned them inside. "Hurry. They're gone."

She gathered up Charity and entered the

apartment, braced for the worst, but she couldn't prevent the gasp that escaped her lips.

The apartment looked like a tornado had attacked. Things weren't just tossed around and upended. Furniture and appliances had been completely dismantled and destroyed. Indentations in the shattered table legs looked like they were made by a bat or something similar.

Clothes had been torn apart, stuffing ripped from fiber-filled winter jackets. Papers floated over everything like snow. Couch cushions and pillows had also been gutted and shaken out, the foam pieces covered every square inch of carpet not already littered with broken furniture pieces.

Charity started to cry, which shook Arissa out of her stunned state so she could softly croon to her niece.

Nathan surprised her then by kneeling next to them and gently rubbing Charity's back. "It's all right," he said to the little girl, then to Arissa, "I'll take her while you look around. See if you can tell if anything's missing."

She coaxed Charity into Nathan's arms, and the little girl seemed to find comfort in his sheltering presence, because her crying dampened to sobs. Arissa wanted to nestle in his strong arms herself, but she managed to stand on shaky legs, grit her teeth and start to pick her way through the chaos.

How in the world would she know if anything had been taken? Even the freezer had been cleaned out, and melted food made the kitchen floor slick. Luckily the fridge was so small that her parents didn't keep much food stored, and her mother's frugal side had caused her to remember to take most of the perishables with them when they'd gone to stay with Mrs. Fuchikami.

The apartment was small, since the area above the grocery store had been divided into two apartments and Arissa's family lived in only one of the units. Her parents' bedroom was as much of a mess as hers, but not as wrecked as the living room and kitchen because there was less stuff in the bedrooms. She stepped over smashed photo frames and some of Charity's broken toys. The dresser drawers had been pulled out and smashed into jagged wooden pieces. Why so much destruction?

Because they were sending a message.

The air in the bedroom seemed thin all of a sudden, and she stepped back out into the living room where Nathan still held a trembling Charity. He looked up at her, and she shook her head, her breath coming in shallow gasps. "I can't tell if…if anything's missing."

"Is there anything you want to take with you?"

She shook her head again, more violently. "There's nothing *left.*"

He searched her face, then stood with Charity in his arms. "Let's get you outside. You're looking pale."

She didn't want to faint in front of Charity, in front of him. She followed him outside to the landing between the two apartment doors. It was a tight squeeze, but the light down below from the window in the door at the base of the stairs made her feel less trapped, less threatened. The door blocked out the sounds of the busy street outside, making the landing a quieter haven than the street, and also set apart from the violence in the apartment.

"I don't know what they'd be looking for," Arissa said in a low voice.

"Something Mark gave you?"

"I was trying to think of something during the drive down to Los Angeles, but I just couldn't think of anything. Christmas or birthday presents were usually gift cards for eating out. Our apartment was so cramped with Mark and me living with Mom and Dad that we didn't have room for much stuff."

"Not even small trinkets?"

"You saw the place. There's no space. Mark had the bedroom and it barely has space for a dresser and bedside table. I slept on the foldout couch in the living room, and I shared the dresser in the bedroom with Mark."

"He didn't...leave anything for Charity?" The way Nathan's voice caught, it almost sounded like he was starting to forgive Mark for his shattered leg.

"If he did, Charity's uncle didn't give it to us when he brought her. All she had was the clothes on her back. No jewelry, no toys. Not even a hairpin."

She smoothed the dark curls from Charity's face. She'd calmed down and now lay with her cheek against Nathan's shoulder, sucking her thumb, her eyes dark and still wet as they looked at Arissa. She'd always been a quiet girl, maybe because of the way she'd been shuttled from one home to another so quickly, so early in her life. Maybe because of what she might have seen in Johnny Capuno's parents' home. While they weren't actively part of the LSLs, their son being a captain had to affect their lives in some way.

"They destroyed our apartment to warn us," Arissa said softly. "To threaten me."

"They also covered up whatever they might have taken from Mark's things," Nathan said.

"No, Mark's things weren't in the apartment."

"What do you mean?"

"It's too small to store anything. After he died—after Internal Affairs released his things to us—we put them in our family storage unit."

He had looked hopeful for a moment, but then he sagged against the wall, his large hand stroking Charity's back. "Then they'd have found out about it by now and searched that, too."

Arissa glanced back at the broken apartment door. "N-no..." she said slowly, "maybe not. The unit isn't in our name."

"Whose name is it in? Mark's?"

"No, we share a large unit that's rented by my aunt Desiree."

Nathan pushed himself away from the wall. "Would the gang members know about it?"

"I don't think so. The bill goes to her, so there's no evidence in the apartment that we use it."

"How about the storage unit key?"

She held up her purse, which still included her key ring, and shook it so that the keys jingled. "When they took me, I dropped my purse. My parents found it on the sidewalk. When we escaped and I went to the grocery store to get my parents out of town, I got it back. My parents have a key, too, but it's with them."

"Then let's go—"

The sound of locks being undone and the doorknob rattling behind Arissa made Nathan's face tighten, and his arms also tightened around Charity. Arissa quickly said, "It's our neighbor."

She turned just as Mrs. Galos opened her apartment door, a smoldering cigarette dangling out of the corner of her mouth. "I thought I heard voices."

"Hi, Mrs. Galos." Arissa was about to introduce Nathan when she realized she probably shouldn't, just in case the gang hadn't yet figured out it was him with her at the rest stop. "Sorry to bother you. We were just leaving." She quickly turned to rush down the stairs and heard Nathan's footsteps following right on her heels.

But she'd forgotten about the broken apartment door. "What kind of trouble are you in?" Mrs. Galos said sharply, her raspy voice grating off the walls of the narrow stairwell. "It scared me to death to hear all the crashing and banging from your apartment."

Arissa glanced back over her shoulder at the older woman. "When did this happen?"

"Yesterday afternoon."

Right after she'd escaped. Had it really been yesterday? Yes, it was, because they'd been attacked at the rest stop late last night.

"I almost called the police." Mrs. Galos's dark gaze shifted away.

Arissa understood why she hadn't. Mrs. Galos must have seen the gang tattoos on the men in the apartment. If she'd called the police, the men trashing the apartment might have figured it was her who had called them. Like anyone else in this neighborhood, Mrs. Galos didn't want any trouble with the gangs.

Understanding fully, Arissa couldn't try

to convince her the men were just robbers. "Just keep your head down," she said to the older woman softly. "They're not interested in you."

Mrs. Galos's lips tightened, then she turned to head back inside her apartment, shaking her head.

Just before her door closed, Charity suddenly said, "Nathan, I need to go to the bathroom."

Arissa tensed at the sound of his name, which she knew Mrs. Galos heard before the door had clicked shut. She looked back up at the closed door, her breath coming faster. Would the gang come back here and question her? Would she tell them that Arissa's friend's name was Nathan? It wouldn't be a huge leap for them to guess that the "Nathan" with her could only be her brother's former partner.

She met Nathan's eyes over Charity's head, and knew he had made the connection, too. But his face tensed and he gestured with his chin for her to keep descending the stairs. There wasn't anything they could do now about Mrs. Galos knowing his name. He spoke softly to the little girl. "We'll stop at a fastfood restaurant so you can go, and we'll get you a snack, too."

The family storage unit wasn't in the best part of town, but the quiet streets did a little to ease the tautness of the muscles across her shoulders. She directed Nathan toward the back of the facility, where the larger units stood. Each had a large roll-up door so that a car could drive into the unit, but Arissa had Nathan park at the far end of the building where there was a walk-in entrance. Once inside, they headed down the long hallway that ran between the two rows of units. Doors flanked them on the left and right, and Arissa went to the seventh on the right. She unlocked the door and flipped on the light as she entered the unit, which was packed with stuff, but neatly organized, closing the door behind her.

"Our things are over here." She walked toward the back right corner, holding Charity's hand in case she decided to poke around at the items at her eye level. She found the boxes in the corner and tried to remember which ones were Mark's. "I think the boxes are marked with my brother's name." She pointed to one, which was unfortunately at the bottom of six others.

Nathan glanced at the stacks, the random pieces of furniture. "This is all yours?" He eyed the two dining room tables, one stacked upside down on top of the other one.

"No, this is—"

Nathan suddenly moved toward her and clapped a hand over her mouth. He also wrapped his arm around Charity's shoulders and pressed her close.

At first all she heard in the silence was the blood pounding in her ears, but then she caught the scrape of metal against metal, a sharp rattle…and then the creak as the walk-in door to this storage unit swung open.

Nathan's fingers against her face twitched. She felt the tendons in his wrist tighten, and she shut her eyes. Then she felt Charity shift against her. She fumbled for her niece and gently covered the girl's mouth with her fingers. Charity trembled.

Booted footsteps clunked against the cement floor, no attempt to be stealthy. Whoever it was didn't know they were there. But for how long? If the intruder walked far enough into the unit, they'd be clearly visible around the legs of the dining room chairs stacked a few feet away.

Nathan's hand fell away and he moved silently toward the intruder. Arissa wanted to keep him here, but instead she tightened her arms around Charity and took a few steps back so that they were behind a covered barbecue grill.

Nathan slid noiselessly behind an empty bookcase and crouched low as the footsteps came closer. Arissa also kneeled, but peeked around the barbecue grill.

Suddenly a blare of classic rock music echoed on the concrete walls. There was a faint clink, as if from a belt buckle, and a rustle of clothing. Then the music abruptly stopped and a man's voice said, "Yeah, what?" It sounded like he was on a cell phone. The booted footsteps stopped, but Nathan's body still radiated tension as he listened.

The intruder grunted into his cell phone, then the steps slowly drew closer to them.

Arissa huddled down, her body closing around Charity. The little girl gave a soft whimper. Arissa peeked out around the base of the grill. A black boot came into view at the same moment she heard the man say, "Yeah, yeah, I know, Mom."

She knew that voice.

Nathan sprang forward.

"Nathan, wait!" She shot to her feet.

Nathan tackled the intruder and crashed into a small end table on top of which rested a fake potted plant only to then land on the floor.

Nathan looked fiercely up at her from where he lay next to Arissa's cousin. Tito's gaze was dazed and disoriented. "Cuz?" he said.

"Tito, what are you doing here?"

"What do you mean? It's Mom's storage unit."

"Un-uncle Tito?" Charity peeked at him from behind Arissa.

"Hey, squirt." But Tito only gave her a

quick affectionate glance before turning back to Arissa. "What's going on?"

At the same time, Nathan demanded, "What's going on?"

Arissa held out a hand to help one of them up from the floor, but Nathan's gaze skittered away from her, so she hauled Tito to his feet.

Nathan had slowly stood. Arissa tried not to show concern at the pain tightening the skin around his eyes as he steadied himself. She knew him well enough to know that he wouldn't welcome any sign of sympathy from her. "Who is this?" His voice came out as a growl, perhaps from his annoyance, perhaps from the pain.

"Nathan, this is my cousin Tito—er, Thomas. We call him Tito. Tito—"

"I know who you are," Tito said, his voice low. "I recognize you from the newspaper photos." When Mark had been killed. Next to Nathan, Tito seemed like a slender reed, although he was a good six inches taller than Arissa and he owed his whipcord-lean body to his marathon running. He glanced, confused, at Arissa, then assessed Nathan with hard eyes. He wasn't quite hostile, but he wasn't overly friendly, either, because he knew, as her whole family did, about how Nathan had reported Mark to Internal Affairs.

"Why are you here?" Nathan asked.

Arissa answered. "The storage unit technically belongs to Tito's mother, my aunt Desiree. To save money, she rents this large unit and then all our extended family shares it, but most of this stuff belongs to my family because our apartment is so small."

Nathan's gaze at Tito was still hard. Arissa had to admit it was a bit coincidental that he'd show up here right after they'd arrived. "Why are you here, Tito?" she asked.

"Mom's Crock-Pot broke. She sent me to pick up her spare, even though I told her I didn't think it was here. I think she gave it to one of the other aunties."

Since Arissa's numerous aunties shared their kitchen appliances and pans freely among themselves, she had a feeling Tito was right—*if* he was telling the truth.

"You're freaking me out, cuz. What's going on?" Tito's brown eyes bored into hers. "Mom tried calling your parents yesterday and the phone kept going straight to voice mail. She's getting worried."

Arissa reached out to touch his wide shoulder, but his muscles bunched at her touch. "They're fine, I promise."

"That's not a good answer."

"That's all the answer you're going to get," Nathan growled, stepping forward.

Tito shot him a sharp look. "Why are you with her? Haven't you done enough to her family?"

It took a second for Arissa to realize Tito was referring to the fact Nathan had reported on Mark to Internal Affairs.

"Nathan's the only one who can help us," Arissa said. "It's fine, Tito."

Her cousin's eyes narrowed as he surveyed Nathan's equally suspicious gaze. "This has something to do with Mark. Why do you need to dig up all the old junk? Just leave it."

"It won't leave me," Arissa said.

Tito's attention snapped back to her. "What do you mean?"

She shouldn't have said anything. "I can't talk about it. The less you know, the better. You shouldn't tell anyone you were here— just borrow a Crock-Pot from one of the other aunties and tell Aunt Desiree you never went to the storage unit."

Now her cousin's expression was anxious for her. "What kind of trouble are you in?"

Charity shifted against her leg, and she reached down to stroke her niece's head. "Just keep your head down, Tito." But shouldn't she warn him? The LSL gang members they grew up with knew Tito was her cousin. "Stay out of the way of the gangs."

His neck muscles pulsed. "Gangs? Arissa, you crossed one of them? You know better than that. Tell me what's going on."

Nathan took another step closer to her. "Look, she already said that the less you know the better."

The two men exchanged more stiff glances before Tito looked away. "Fine." He reached out a hand and stroked Charity's soft cheek.

"Watch yourself, cuz. And keep Charity safe, too."

"Nathan will keep us safe," she said.

At the same time, Nathan said, "She has me to keep them safe."

There was an awkward silence, then Tito reached out to give Arissa a buss on the cheek, and he bent to give Charity a smacking kiss, too. "See you."

But before he walked away, his eyes slid to the stacks of boxes in the corner that contained her family's things—and Mark's things, too.

Then the door to the storage unit opened and shut, and he was gone.

Nathan went to make sure he'd left, returning with a grim nod. "Is that typical? Does his mother often send him to the storage unit for things?"

"Sort of. She sends him to the storage unit a few times a year, but her house is larger than ours and she doesn't often need anything here. My family comes to the storage unit more often since more of our stuff is here."

Nathan gave Charity a careful look before saying, "It seemed odd he'd show up like this."

"Tito's the youngest of his family and he's still living at home, although he insists on paying rent. His mom sends him on errands all the time. He's always been a good son." She paused. "He and Mark weren't that close, but he's been good to me since Mark died. And he loves Charity."

But Nathan's face hadn't lost any of its wariness. She couldn't blame him. In all her years of going to the storage unit for things for her parents, she'd never run into Tito here. Until today, of all days. Was it really coincidence? But she didn't want to believe Tito could be involved in this. He couldn't be.

Nathan turned away from her. "Let's hurry and look through Mark's things." He hefted the topmost box from the stack she'd pointed out earlier. They dragged out the one box labeled as Mark's on the bottom, but it ended up being full of Mark's clothes. Nathan went through each item, but there was nothing, not even pocket change.

"Internal Affairs went through everything. I doubt there's anything he left behind that they haven't examined." Arissa folded a shirt and placed it back in the box. The scent of her brother, that comforting mix of soap and his cologne, caused a weight against her rib cage.

Another box wasn't Mark's, but it had some old dolls that had probably belonged to one of her cousins. Arissa gratefully gave them to Charity to play with nearby while they continued to search.

They found a second box filled with Mark's papers—old tax returns, bills, credit card statements. "Let's take this with us." Nathan set it aside.

Arissa didn't think they'd find anything. Internal Affairs had gone through all that, too. They found more things, including a box full of random stuff. "This was in the bedside table next to Mark's bed."

Nathan stopped and looked at her. "You

said he slept in the bedroom, you slept in the living room?"

She blinked in surprise. "Yes, on the fold-out couch."

He looked stunned. "You...you had that fancy condo."

"How did you know?"

"Mark took me by once because he had to give something to you, but you weren't home, so he left it in your mailbox." Nathan licked his lips, glanced back at the box. "I know you said you and Mark gave up your apartments after your mom got sick, but it just didn't register to me, I guess, how cramped it was in your parents' place."

Arissa turned away and watched Charity play with the old dolls. "Mom needed the money," she said softly. "Mark and I didn't mind."

The silence between them was strained, somehow, so she turned back to the box. "There isn't anything else, I think."

"Let's take this with us, too, just in case." Nathan rose and hefted a box back onto the stack, but his leg trembled from crouching for so long, and the one he held tilted. A few pieces of mail drifted out.

Arissa picked them up and looked at them. "Are these bills? Why didn't Dad open these?" She flipped through them, sighing. "This is junk mail. Mom would have a fit. She hates it when Dad stores useless stuff that should be tossed out."

But Nathan's eyes stayed fixed on the envelopes. "Arissa, did Mark get any mail after he died? Anything IA didn't see?"

She stilled. She hadn't thought of that. "Yes, we were always getting things addressed to him. It upset Mom to see the envelopes, so Dad just threw them in a box. Most of it was junk mail, but he wouldn't throw it away because it was Mark's—I can kind of understand. I knew about the box and could have thrown it out, but I didn't want to."

"What happened to it?"

She thought back. The box of unopened junk mail had been tucked inside the bedside table in Mark's bedroom—now where she and Charity slept. It had sat there for months, but she hadn't known when her father had taken it away. She had just looked inside the bedside table one day and it was gone. "Dad must have taken it here. It's got to be somewhere."

"What does it look like?" Nathan began taking down boxes and looking through them.

"It's a shoe box." She closed her eyes for a moment to picture it. "Nike. Orange. Mark had bought new running shoes a week before he died. We saw them in the box of his clothes."

Nathan nodded.

"The shoe box was still in Mark's bedroom, so Dad started throwing his mail into it."

They had to go through almost every box, but they eventually found it. She spotted the bright orange color and pulled it out, flipping open the lid. The first envelope was a magazine renewal reminder, addressed to Mark. "This is it."

"Let's bring it with us." Nathan took the

shoe box from her and put it with the box of Mark's papers.

They restacked the boxes and Arissa gathered up some of the dolls Charity had been playing with. She figured that whichever cousin they had once belonged to wouldn't mind, since all her cousins were now past the age to play with them.

Nathan winced as he bent to pick up one of the boxes, and Arissa knew he'd never admit his leg was paining him. "Why don't you drive the car around to this side?" She pointed to the roll-up metal door next to them, which was on the opposite side of the unit as the door they'd come in. "I can roll the door up and we can load the boxes easier."

He looked at her for a long moment. She thought he might refuse her at first, but she only wanted to help him without making him feel like an invalid. She understood his pride and his frustration, but there was no need for him to deliberately make things harder on himself. The truth was, he'd been injured in the line of duty, and that was honorable. He had nothing to prove, not to her.

Did he somehow sense her thoughts? He nodded, but it wasn't a curt, frustrated jerk of the head. Instead, it seemed like he had a softer, grateful look in his green-gray eyes.

Arissa quickly unlatched the door and pulled it up with a loud rattle that echoed off the concrete walls. Nathan ducked outside and went to his SUV, driving it back to the unit. They loaded the two boxes of Mark's things into the back and slammed the trunk closed.

As Arissa reached up to pull the metal rolling door closed again, she caught the growl of a modified car engine. Glancing to the side, she saw a lowered sedan with a custom paint job creep around the far corner of the building.

She froze. It was too far away for her to see clearly, but something about the man in the driver's seat seemed familiar. And the souped-up car itself reminded her of the custom rides that the LSL members drove through her neighborhood.

The driver turned toward her, and the car paused for a moment.

Arissa stared at him. She couldn't place him. Was he an LSL gang member? Or was she mistaken? Her heartbeat began to pick up. He was alone. He wouldn't do anything to them, would he? How would the LSLs know Arissa would be here?

Then suddenly the muscle car sped off with a roar of its engine, which reverberated off of the concrete and metal of the storage facility.

"Get in the car, now." Nathan's voice was tight.

"Was that one of the LSL gang?" Arissa grabbed Charity and plunked her in her safety seat. "Did you recognize him?"

"No, I didn't." Nathan started the engine. "But his actions were suspicious. We need to get out of here fast."

As they exited the storage facility's driveway, Arissa looked around at the street. No sign of the custom car or the man. In fact, the street was as quiet as it had been when they arrived.

Nathan scanned the street, too, but its emptiness didn't make him relax. He headed out and kept his eyes moving, searching the side streets, examining the cars.

"Who was he?" Arissa whispered.

"I don't know. I don't even know if he was LSL."

"I didn't get a good look at him, he was too far away. I couldn't see much, although he seemed young."

"He could be a wannabe, hoping to get into the gang."

In which case, he might tell the gang what he'd seen, trying to curry favor. "Would he know they're after me? Would they have told someone who wasn't in the gang about me?"

"I doubt it. We don't know for sure that he's not an LSL. I haven't been in Narcotics for three years."

There was tightness in his voice, and she dropped the subject.

They had almost reached the end of the street where it T-junctioned with a busier boulevard when Nathan expelled a breath, almost a laugh. "Look." He pointed to the street corner.

Arissa tensed when she saw the custom car parked on the curb, but then she saw the group of women gathered together, and with them was the young driver. What she'd thought was a young man was actually a young woman, not wearing any makeup, her smooth dark hair pulled back in a braid down her back. She wore a sleeveless T-shirt under a dark vest, with piercings and tattoos on her face and one side of her neck, but her figure was unmistakably female and she wore high-heeled leather boots. Her friends, laughing with her, were dressed in leather and studs, and a couple had on chaps. There were a few Harley-Davidsons parked on the street nearby and she guessed some of the women had ridden them to this gathering. The women started making their way toward the door of a bar a few feet away.

Arissa let out a breath. "I feel stupid."

"I feel stupider." Nathan gave her a side look and a half smile, his face transformed into the adventurous, teasing Nathan she'd known before.

She couldn't help smiling back, but then suddenly it was as if his face was a window slammed shut, and he concentrated on driving again.

Arissa turned to look out the passenger window, not seeing a thing, her teeth digging into her lip. His refusal to share the moment with her was a good reminder. This was the man who had accused her brother, who blamed him for the loss of his career, who seemed to persist in his suspicions even after IA had cleared Mark. This was just another man who had abandoned her, and she had to remember that. Besides, if she and Charity had to disappear, she'd never see him again, so why let him get too close to her?

Her heart hurt. She held tightly to her pain as they drove out of Los Angeles, determined to never let Nathan hurt her again.

FIVE

Nathan tried to focus on the long stretch of road as they drove through central California, heading north. Arissa didn't say a word.

When he'd known her before, she hadn't been a chatterer, but she'd always made him laugh with random comments or funny stories about her work. Her silence now seemed strange. She'd withdrawn from him.

He ought to be glad about it. He'd been getting too comfortable with her. He wanted to protect her because she had no one else to help her, and he wanted to know what Mark had been up to that would cause the LSLs to come after her three years following his death, but Nathan also didn't want to get close to her again. His attraction to her was too strong, and with Charity to take care of, she needed someone whole. Not someone like him.

But he wanted to hear her talking to him. Her low voice always seemed to touch something inside him that made him feel more at ease, even when she was disagreeing with him.

"Can you trust Tito?" he blurted. As soon as the words were out of his mouth, even before she turned wide eyes to him, he wanted to give himself a smack upside the head. What was he doing? He knew better than to bring up a difficult topic. He cleared his throat. "I don't want to accuse him of anything—"

"That would be a first," she muttered and looked away again.

He supposed he deserved that. "The fact he showed up at the storage unit is bothering me."

Her scowl disappeared, but her lips were still tight. "I thought about that, too."

"Would he have joined the LSLs and not told you? Because of Mark?"

She thought about it for a long moment.

"No, I don't think so. We both know gang members—you can't avoid it when you grow up in our neighborhood—but Tito never had any interest in joining the gang when he was younger. I can't see why he'd suddenly want to join them now."

"I guess if he was an LSL, he wouldn't have just walked into the storage unit. He'd have called for someone to meet him there, or he'd have tried to stall us."

"What bothered me was that he was so persistent in trying to figure out what had happened to me, almost as if he wanted to know what I was going to do."

Nathan had thought Tito seemed pushy, but wasn't sure if that was his personality. "He isn't usually like that?"

"Well…Tito was concerned about me, which might explain it. He's protective of the people he cares about. He's a bit like you." Then her face flushed, and she looked away.

It took him a moment to understand that her comment implied he was protecting her and Charity because he cared about them. He coughed lightly. Not going to go there.

"You're close to him?" That seemed a neutral enough question.

"You probably already know that my entire extended family is close, but Tito and I got a lot closer after Mark died. It was as if he wanted to watch out for me since Mark couldn't anymore. All of us have drawn closer because of his death. Everyone's always checking in on my parents now, more often than they did before."

"Didn't they rally around your mom when she had her cancer diagnosis? I remember..." His words caught, but he recovered quickly. "I remember Mark told me about it."

"You're right, they did. But they really bonded together after the funeral."

"How's your mom doing these days?" Guilt twinged in his stomach that he hadn't asked her about her mom before. He had been with Mark when his partner had gotten the phone call about the cancer. He'd never seen Mark look so sick.

"She's great. It's in remission. She's living life more adventurously than she used to."

He could understand why.

Arissa continued, "I wish we had the money so that she could do the things on her bucket list."

He remembered the tiny apartment and what Arissa had revealed about herself and Mark giving up their apartments to live with their parents. "You've still got medical bills to pay?"

She nodded. "And the grocery store isn't doing very well these days. If we didn't have Mark's pension…" She glanced at him, then swallowed.

He focused on the semi in front of them, then checked his mirrors to pass it. Because of him, they'd almost lost that income. But he couldn't have lied about what he'd seen. And at the time, his anger and bitterness had gouged a hole in his spirit, and he'd wanted someone to pay for that bullet in his leg.

Did he still blame Mark? He wasn't sure anymore. Not after seeing how Mark and Arissa had been trying to help her family. Was that why Mark had become a mole, to help pay medical bills? "It must have been hard, living with your parents and Mark."

"It was cramped, but it wasn't too hard. I got to spend more time with my family than I had in years."

He knew it wasn't just her job as an international flight attendant that had kept her from spending time with her family. Mark had spoken freely about his concern for Arissa. Before her mom's cancer, she had been irresponsible, staying out late and hanging with a wild crowd. Mark had been worried about her.

But then their mom got sick, and Arissa had changed. And it wasn't just Mark telling him. Nathan had seen it, too. She'd gone from a carefree party girl to a worried daughter. Whenever he'd seen her, she'd had a shadow behind her eyes where before had only been a carefree light. It was as if she'd matured in a single day.

And Nathan had fallen head over heels for her.

He'd been attracted to her before, despite her fondness for raves and dancing, despite her lack of Christian faith. But this new Arissa, closer to her brother, more concerned and responsible for her mother—she'd been even harder for him to resist. He'd wanted to gather her close and shelter her from all the troubles in her life. He'd wanted to help her through them.

Which was why when she'd visited him at the hospital, he'd said such cutting things and ruthlessly sent her away. She was the one woman he wanted, and yet he couldn't have her. It wasn't just because her brother had betrayed him—Mark's mistakes weren't her fault. It was because at the time Nathan hadn't known if he'd ever walk again and he refused to burden a woman with something like that. So he'd lashed out at her.

And now, with time and distance, he could see how hurtful he'd been to someone who was going through her own grieving. "I'm sorry." His voice was hoarse.

She blinked at him. "For what?"

"That day you visited me in the hospital."

Her entire face turned to marble—cold, still and carefully neutral.

"I'm sorry for hurting you," he continued. "I'm sorry for lashing out at you."

"I understand." A flash of cynicism cracked the smoothness of her face. "Your leg was shattered. Of course you didn't want to see me, the sister of your dead partner who you blamed for your injury." While her words should have been gentle, they were bitter.

They drove in silence for a while. He didn't know what to say. He didn't know why he'd thought apologizing would suddenly make everything better.

Then she spoke in a low voice. "Nathan, for so long I thought I'd be angry at you for reporting what you'd seen to Internal Affairs, for continuing to believe Mark was a mole."

Very nicely, she didn't say, *Despite the lack of evidence.* Even though he believed what he'd seen at the chop shop, the fact that Arissa doubted him stung deeply.

"I didn't want to ask for your help," she continued. "I knew you'd want nothing more to do with us. But as soon as I heard Mark's name, I also knew you were the only one who could help me, and I had to come to you." She turned to him, her eyes a mix of sadness, hardness and tiredness. "And now it's starting to look like Mark was doing something suspicious, so how can I be angry at you for reporting what you'd seen when you might have been right?" Her mouth firmed. "But it doesn't make me any less angry that you stayed away from us. Did you think we were involved in Mark's business, too?"

"No, of course not." But a nagging part of him admitted that he'd suspected it. He'd been so betrayed, he hadn't wanted to have anything to do with the Tiong family. That, and he'd wanted to avoid Arissa with her soulful eyes and scent of rain and roses.

He swallowed. "I was—" *Broken.* "—in pain. I didn't want to see anyone. And then when I was on the road to recovery, so much time had passed, and your brother was gone…"

Arissa tucked her feet up under her as she sat on the seat, her cheek against the chair back at she looked at him. "Mark might have been a mole," she whispered. "I can't believe it."

He wouldn't have believed it either if he

hadn't seen Mark give that copy of the police case file to the LSL gang member.

"He wasn't always a bad cop, was he?" Arissa asked.

"No. Arissa, he was my best friend." *And I never knew him.* "He was a great cop. We were a great team."

She didn't respond, just stared off in the direction of his hands on the steering wheel.

Nathan said, "There was one time we cornered a drug dealer. Peppi Indigo was a coward, everyone knew it, but he was smart. He'd avoided prison because he was afraid of it. But Mark and I caught him red-handed with a trunk full of heroine."

Dawn had been a faint blush in the sky when they'd trapped Peppi in the empty parking garage. Los Angeles hadn't even begun to wake up yet—or the other lowlifes were just getting to bed. He and Mark had been dead tired from being up all night, and they'd gotten a little punch-drunk while staking out Peppi's car. That was the only reason Nathan could think of why they'd done what they did.

"We caught Peppi in a drug deal. We'd been watching him and we came out a little aggressively, guns hot. I got the buyer down on the ground and Mark grabbed Peppi. But we were tired, and we'd forgotten how desperate men can do desperate things. Peppi managed to wrestle with Mark and knock away his gun. Peppi had your brother in front of him as a human shield."

She gasped, and he winced. He was such a chump; he wasn't supposed to alarm her.

"It wasn't for long," he said quickly. "Mark looked right at me and mouthed 'Prudence.'"

"Huh?"

"Prudence was the name of a woman down in Human Resources. She wasn't a very big woman, but for some reason every time she sat down in her chair, she'd drop down hard like a dive-bomber. Mark and I commented about it between ourselves all the time."

"What did he mean by saying her name?"

"I wasn't entirely sure, but I had a guess. Then he put his hand up to his chest with three fingers showing. It was only a few seconds, but Peppi had started shouting at me to drop my weapon and he was waving his own piece around like a madman. Mark counted off with his fingers—three, two, one. Then Mark threw his elbow backward into Peppi's jaw and dropped to the ground so fast that Peppi didn't know what was going on."

"Prudence the dive-bomber," Arissa murmured.

"I injured Peppi and then Mark disarmed him."

"You saved his life," Arissa said.

"I doubt Peppi would have shot him, not a cop. Then he'd really be in trouble and Peppi was too smart and too much of a coward to do that."

Her eyes on him were still solemn, despite his reassurance. "You're right, you two were a good team."

Once. Before that chop shop. Before Mark had started doing what Nathan suspected he had been doing—selling out the LAPD in order to pay for his mother's cancer treatments.

He took the route through Oakland and then into Sonoma. As they began to see farm fields and vineyards, Nathan found that the sight eased the rock-hard muscles in his neck.

Home. He was going home.

He hadn't felt like Sonoma was home in a long time. It had been the place of his failure, because he came back to Sonoma no longer a cop. But now after living there for three years, working with a Sonoma physical therapist, getting a job at a condominium building just outside of downtown Sonoma, the surroundings had become familiar. Calming.

The thought of going back to live in Los Angeles caused a pang of unease. No, he couldn't do it. Not just because of the memories, not just because he couldn't belong to the LAPD anymore, but because it wasn't *home* to him.

"It's beautiful here." The last thin rays of sunlight through the fir trees lining the highway made dappled patterns on Arissa's face. "I don't know how you left here to work in L.A."

If he hadn't gotten shot, he would still be down south, facing the danger of the streets rather than the soothing scent of cherry trees in bloom. It was almost enough to trick him into thinking it was a good thing he'd been forced to move back home. As if it had had a purpose. As if the shoot-out at the chop shop had been part of a larger plan.

That was stupid. There was no God, no higher power controlling any of it. God had abandoned Nathan in that chop shop. End of story.

Night had just fallen as he drove outside of downtown Sonoma, turning into a driveway lined with hedges on one side and duplexes on the other.

"Where are we?" Arissa looked around at the row of small rentals, which seemed to be surrounded by fields of grapevines. "I can't believe I hadn't even thought to ask you. I knew we weren't going back to your parents' house."

"I hadn't thought much about it until we were in central California." Nathan pulled in front of one of the duplexes. "When you were at a rest stop with Charity, I called Liam O'Neill."

"Who's he?"

"His older brother Shaun is a good friend of mine." Nathan stopped in front of the third duplex down the line and cut the engine. "Liam just got back from a tour in Afghanistan, but not many people know he's home again." The only reason Nathan knew was because Shaun had mentioned it last week.

"This is his home?" Arissa took in the whitewashed wooden walls, the three steps up to a door with a ripped screen. "Won't people be able to track where he lives?"

"No, this is just a place he's renting." Nathan got out of the car, and Arissa did also. "He's left the army on medical discharge, so he's trying to start up a new skip-tracing business." Another reason to bring Arissa and Charity here—if things got bad, Liam could help them escape off the grid so the gang couldn't find them. Nathan noticed the beat-up pickup truck in the carport. "He got a new car."

Arissa eyed the car, then looked at Nathan, but didn't say anything as she opened the back door to unbelt Charity from her safety seat.

He went around the car. "Here, let me carry her." He stepped close to take the sleeping little girl from Arissa's arms.

Time stopped. All he saw were Arissa's eyes, dark and shining up at him. He smelled rain and roses mingled with cherry blossoms, freshly overturned dirt, and honeysuckle from a vine climbing near the duplex window.

The moonlight gilded her face with pearl dust. She was like a vision he expected to melt away. She should step away from him— why didn't she? Then he realized he had trapped her against the car.

So he took advantage of that and leaned in and kissed her.

Her lips were soft and warm rather than cold, and he suddenly heard the crickets in the bushes, the faint hoot of an owl, all circling them in together. He was with Arissa, he was holding Charity in his arms, and it was as if the three of them belonged together, fitted together like puzzle pieces. This was where he wanted to be, kissing Arissa and holding her child and being a part of their family.

The sagging lightbulb over the front door suddenly flickered to life, and he broke away from her. Her face was now bathed in the sickly yellow from the bulb, but she looked at him with eyes both dazed and also longing.

Yes, he felt that way, too.

He shouldn't. This was the last woman in the world he could feel this way with. She knew too much about him. She knew who he had been, and could compare it with who he was now.

Nathan turned toward the front door just as Liam O'Neill unlocked the inner wooden door and pushed open the screen door. "Hi, Nathan." His voice was deep and soft, so low that the crickets almost drowned him out.

"Liam, this is Arissa and Charity."

"Come on in, quick in case someone sees you." He swung the screen door wider.

Nathan should have thought of that before

drowning in Arissa's eyes and scent and giving in to the insane urge to kiss her.

Carrying Charity, he entered the small home, walking straight into Liam's living room and apparently his office, since there was no furniture other than a table and chair with a laptop computer on it and a mess of wires on the floor.

"Take her into the bedroom." Liam gestured to the door in the far wall.

Nathan entered the dark room and fumbled on the wall for the light switch. The ceiling light looked new, and the soft glow illuminated a tiny room with only a mattress on the floor. Liam had made it up with new sheets and a stack of blankets was folded up at the foot. Nathan pulled back the top sheet and laid Charity down, covering her and smoothing the dark hair out of her eyes. Her thumb was loosely in her mouth, but her jaw hung open with her lower lip tucked in, just like her father when he slept.

Suddenly, seeing Mark's face in his daughter made Nathan miss him in a fierce rush. He squeezed his eyes shut for a moment, then leaned down to kiss Charity's cheek. He put a blanket over her and turned off the light, but left the door ajar.

Arissa had opened the car trunk and now set one of the boxes on the floor of Liam's living room, followed by Liam with the other box. Nathan felt in his pocket for the car keys and pressed the button to arm the alarm, seeing the SUV headlights flicker through the large living room window, which was curtained only by some dingy sheer panels.

Nathan studied his surroundings. The kitchen was at the other end of the room, a section of linoleum that started where the scratched hardwood floors ended. There was a back door from the kitchen. Other than the bedroom door, there wasn't much else to the duplex.

Arissa looked around also, and frowned. "Are we taking your only bedroom?"

Liam shifted his shoulder, where the angry red scars from his surgery puckered out of the skin, clearly visible because of the sleeveless shirt he wore. "I don't sleep much," he said in a clipped voice. For the first time, Nathan noticed how thin his face was. His buzz cut only emphasized the tightness of the skin around his wide jaw and prominent cheekbones, but his dark blue eyes were fiercely independent.

Nathan knew how he felt. Wounded warriors, both of them. The nightmares would go away eventually—maybe he'd get a little help from counseling, like Nathan had.

But Arissa eyed him, unimpressed. "What, you're going to sleep upright in your chair?"

Liam blinked at her. "Uh…"

"We'll be fine with blankets out here in the living room," Nathan interjected.

"I've got extra pillows in the bedroom closet," Liam added.

Arissa frowned at the hardwood floor. "No, that'll still be too uncomfortable. Maybe we should try to find somewhere else."

"My duplex neighbor is out of town," Liam said. "He asked me to keep an eye on his place. I can call him and ask if Nathan and I can sleep over there."

"That still means one of you is on the

floor with blankets, only next door instead of here."

Liam smiled then, and Nathan caught a glimpse of the young man he'd once been, before he'd gone to war. "Mr. Brummel has a fold-out couch."

"That'll work." Arissa looked at the two of them. "Are you sure it's all right?"

"Positive." Liam seemed to stand a little taller as he said, "With the two of us here, no one will be able to hurt you and Charity."

Nathan realized what he'd done in calling Liam, because it was what he'd have felt in Liam's place—he'd given him someone to protect. After losing that role because of his accident in Afghanistan, he'd needed to feel like a protector again. And Nathan knew that Liam wouldn't allow anything to happen to Arissa or Charity.

After Liam called his neighbor to make sure it was all right for them to bunk there, he led the way outside and up the front steps of the other apartment of the duplex. Before leaving for Los Angeles this morning, Nathan had grabbed a small overnight bag at his parents' house and he carried it with him as he followed Liam next door.

However as he walked up the three steps to the front door, his leg suddenly wobbled and gave way.

As he stumbled, pain splintered up his leg, stabbing needles into his hip. His hand slammed out against the house wall to steady himself, and he squeezed his eyes shut and grit his teeth against the agony in his leg.

"You okay?" Liam's voice was gruff, as if unsure if he ought to be concerned or not.

"Fine. I've just been sitting for too long." Nathan had tried to stretch his legs each time they'd stopped along the drive, but after driving to and from Los Angeles in one day, his leg muscles were weak and twitchy.

Liam bent and picked up the duffel bag Nathan had dropped, then silently carried it inside for him—didn't ask, didn't say anything, didn't show sympathy. Nathan was glad.

He stayed outside a moment, breathing in the honeysuckle, one hand still braced against the house and the other massaging his leg, although it didn't stop the pain. The bone ached deep inside with a sharp, rolling torture that no amount of massage could ease.

Half a man. He was barely half a man. Why did Arissa come to him when he couldn't even walk up three steps into a house? Why did she have to look at him as if she completely trusted him to protect her and Charity, when he wasn't sure he could even protect himself? He shouldn't be doing this. He shouldn't be near her, he shouldn't be helping her. She'd disrupted the calm, peaceful place he'd found after realizing what his leg would never be able to do ever again. She made him feel things he'd rather not be feeling.

In so many ways, she was the last person he should get close to. He'd been the one to suspect her brother was a mole. That brother had been the reason he'd been shot and injured. And that injury made him feel somehow set apart from other men, set apart from normal relationships. And worst of all, his injury might end up getting them hurt or killed.

A deep sliver of fear inside him whispered that he was only setting himself up to fail them all.

SIX

When Nathan returned from putting away his bag, Arissa noticed a tightness around his eyes, even though he avoided looking at her.

It was just as well. Their kiss had made her feel like she'd been bucked off a horse—exhilarating, but painful when crashing back to reality.

When he'd taken Charity from her, she hadn't wanted to move away from his nearness. She could smell his musk and lime, mingled with honeysuckle, and it filled her lungs, making her not want to exhale. The strong column of his throat had gleamed in the moonlight while his jaw, shadowed, had seemed softer, vulnerable. She hadn't been able to see his eyes clearly, but she'd felt their gaze on her face, and she couldn't look away. She'd wanted him to draw nearer to her, and when he did, she had lifted her lips to meet his.

His kiss made the ground drop from under her feet. Even though his arms weren't around her, she somehow felt as if they were anchoring her. It had been the three of them in a sheltering circle, a place set apart from the rest of the world, a place where she could open herself up to him and never be hurt.

She had been about to reach up to touch his cheek when the light had gone on and Liam had opened the door. The way he broke away from her had been like a slap.

But really, she couldn't blame him. Why would he want to get more deeply involved with her than he already was? She'd put his family in danger. She had a three-year-old whose parents had been involved in one way or another with a ruthless drug gang. He hadn't had to work today because of the double shift he'd pulled the day before, but she couldn't keep him from his job forever. He needed to get rid of her and Charity and get back to his life, without drug gangs and bullets like the one that shattered his career.

But a part of her dreamed of a world where he'd look at her the way he had before the day at the chop shop. She'd seen a shadow of that look tonight, but now it was completely erased from his face.

Liam had gone out to the garage and found a couple more folding chairs for them to sit on in his bare living room. Nathan now sank into one with a grimace that he quickly smoothed from his face. He glanced at her, as if worried she'd seen his pain, then quickly looked away.

He didn't want her to worry about his injury. Worry...or *pity?*

The realization startled her, but she shouldn't have been surprised. He was like Mark had been—confident when he was healthy and fit, but somehow emotionally damaged when he was physically injured or ill.

Well, she'd lived in close proximity to her brother. She definitely knew how to handle Nathan.

She glanced at the time on her cell phone—nearly nine o'clock. "Did you eat dinner yet?" she asked Liam. "I can cook if you've got food." She headed to the small, practically vintage fridge and was pleasantly surprised to see it stocked.

"Shaun's girlfriend, Monica, came by yesterday with groceries for me." Liam spoke from over her shoulder, sounding a bit sheepish. "I've been making peanut butter sandwiches for the week I've been back."

"I can whip up something." Arissa reached for the broccoli and flank steak. A stir fry would feed them all and be fast. "Got any rice?"

He pointed to one of the cabinets near the floor. "Monica brought a bag."

She started the rice in a pot on the stove and then made a stir fry of slices of beef with chunks of vegetables, flavored with hot pepper flakes. She could have wished for some other sauces to flavor it with, but Liam's cupboards were sparse.

Nathan and Liam sifted through the box of Mark's papers while she worked, and she took the time to calm her emotions, walling them away. The kiss had never happened. He obviously regretted it and she wasn't about to embarrass him or herself by making it a big deal. It was an aberration brought on by moonlight and honeysuckle.

But when she brought the food to them, bowls of rice with the stir fry spooned on top, Nathan's fingers covered hers when he reached for his bowl. She almost thought his touch lingered on hers before he pulled away his meal, nearly spilling a piece of broccoli from the edge of the bowl. "Thanks," he said.

"Smells good." Liam dug into the food with gusto, making Arissa wonder if he hadn't had a home-cooked meal in a while.

She sank into a chair with her own serving and asked, "Liam, why aren't you staying with your dad? Or one of your brothers?"

"Michael's up north in Mendocino, and I didn't want to live there. Too far away from Dad. Brady's wife is nice, but she…" He waved his hand in a fluttering motion. "…worries about me a lot."

Arissa bit back a smile but understood his feelings. Mark was the same way when Mom worried about any injuries he got on the job. While he'd loved his mom fiercely, it hadn't prevented him from being tired out by her hovering.

"Dad twisted his knee a few months ago and since Shaun's still living with him, he's helping take care of him." Liam shrugged. "I didn't want to be in the way."

"It's a good thing he's not living with his family," Nathan said gruffly. "So no one else knows he's here. It's a safer place for us to stay."

Arissa set down her bowl in her lap. "I just don't want to bring trouble on you, too."

"You won't," Liam said. "The gang won't find you here because even if they're watching Nathan's family to see if he'd hid with them, no one else knows I'm back from Afghanistan, and most people would probably expect me to stay with one of my family."

True—after all, *she* had expected it.

"If we can determine why the gang wants you, and what Mark was up to, we can plan what to do next," Nathan said. "Staying with Liam will be safe for a while, but if it comes to it, Liam can help you and Charity disappear."

He avoided her eye as he said it. He was probably looking forward to getting her out of his hair, one way or another.

But like Nathan's father had told her, she and Charity needed to figure out what the gang was after. Otherwise, they would be on the run, maybe for the rest of their lives. And her family might still be in danger. The situation seemed to drain something from inside her, leaving her weak and trembling. Why was this happening to her? Why couldn't Mark's secrets have stayed in the past?

Why did it feel like God had abandoned her?

She had to keep Charity safe, no matter what. She had to do this. She just didn't know if she had the strength to. She was grateful for Nathan and Liam's help, but ultimately she had to find inner reserves to get herself and Charity through this—and she was starting to run dry.

She was so tired. She felt so alone.

She did her best to shake off the sense of helplessness. "Let's hope it doesn't come to that. Have you found anything?"

They continued going through the box until finally it was time to go to bed, but found nothing unusual. Sometimes Liam or Nathan would show her something, and while she tried to keep her suspicions high and see if it might be something more than it seemed, they couldn't find anything concrete they could act on.

His old credit card statements were vague. Meals at Filipino restaurants—well, she ate there, too, because they were near her parents' store. No huge purchases except one $250 purchase at Macy's—but it was the day before her mom's birthday, and she seemed to recall she and Mark and her dad pooling their money for a gift certificate for Mom one year. There was a large bill at a garage when Mark's car had been relatively new and problem-free, but Arissa noticed it was the garage her father always used, and she remembered her father's truck had needed a new muffler.

"The day Mark died..." Arissa paused. While it didn't upset her as much now, she had a feeling it might upset Nathan. However, he nodded for her to continue. "The day Mark died, Dad was driving Mark's car to take Mom to and from the hospital."

Nathan's brow knit, and then his eyebrows rose. "Yes, that day, Mark was driving that ancient little Escort you used to have."

"How do you remember that?"

He hesitated, then said quietly, "I followed him to the chop shop, remember?"

Mark's betrayal settled on her shoulders, guilt and pain mingled together. Focus, she had to focus. She shook off the feeling and kept looking through the papers in her lap.

Long after Nathan and Liam had gone next door to go to sleep, she lay next to Charity, hearing her soft breathing, but feeling more alone than ever. She almost asked God if He were there...but she kept her thoughts to herself. She didn't want to doubt God, but what she felt right now scared her because it felt like doubt.

The next morning, Charity awoke early and Arissa started a pot of coffee in the empty kitchen. She found some oatmeal in the cupboards and made breakfast for herself and her niece, then settled her on the mattress in the bedroom with the dolls they'd taken from the storage unit yesterday.

By that time, Liam and Nathan entered the house and she made breakfast for them, as well. Then they went back to work—tedious work that began to make her vision swim with numbers and names. This time, she offered to go through Mark's personal email account. Internal Affairs had looked through it, also, in addition to his LAPD email account, but Nathan wanted to cover all the bases, and she happened to know Mark's password. It didn't take her more than an hour—Mark had mostly used his LAPD address, so his personal email account had very little besides a few newsletters and messages from herself or her cousins.

"Nothing." She sat back in the folding

chair in front of Liam's laptop computer and rubbed her eyes.

"Did you check his sent folder?" Nathan looked up from the credit card statement he was poring over.

"Yes. Nothing looked strange. He mostly emailed me or our family."

"How about school friends or work colleagues?" Liam said. "Someone you wouldn't know personally."

She shook her head. "He used this email almost entirely for family, and his work one for everything else. There are a few to and from Nathan, but I think he mostly used his work email address when messaging you."

Nathan nodded. "I got the fastest response if I used his work rather than his personal email address."

"I did, too. He only checked his personal account once a week or so." She sighed and stared at Liam's computer screen. "Do we really think this will get us anywhere? Internal Affairs saw all this and didn't find anything."

"What *didn't* Internal Affairs see?" Liam asked.

"That batch of junk mail." She reached into the other box and pulled out the orange shoebox.

They began slitting open the envelopes, even when it was obvious it was pure junk mail—credit card applications, sweepstakes, magazine subscription renewals.

"Did he actually get these magazines?" Nathan asked.

Good question. She stared at the renewals. "Yes. I remember seeing all of them."

She opened an envelope that looked like another credit card application, but upon reading it, froze. "Nathan." Her voice came out sounding strangled.

It was a letter from First Sonoma Bank. Not a credit card application, but a notice that payment for his safe deposit box was due and if he didn't return payment with the attached stub, payment would be deducted from his checking account at no charge to him.

Nathan's brows flattened over his eyes,

which turned a stormy gray. "First Sonoma Bank?"

"He didn't have a Sonoma bank account as far as I knew."

"It's an...unusual bank," Liam said.

"Unusual how?" Arissa asked.

Nathan replied, "It's not very vigilant about asking for identification papers or social security numbers, so a lot of illegal immigrants use it."

"So it would be a good place for a man with secrets." Arissa looked at the paper. Here was definite proof Mark had been hiding something from her, and while it should have pained her, she only felt numb.

"We need to get access to his safe deposit box." Nathan took the page from her and read it again. "He obviously rented it for a reason."

"Do you think they'd let me access it since Charity's his daughter? I have my guardianship papers in my wallet—I needed them recently when I added her to my health insurance."

"It's worth a shot." Nathan rose. "Let's go. We'll take Charity with us, just in case."

First Sonoma Bank was actually on the outskirts of Sonoma, an old building that had once been a Wells Fargo that had closed down. The landscaping looked like it had been grand at one point but now looked scraggly, and the stucco on the walls was dingy. The front glass doors, rusted and a little battered-looking, didn't swing very easily and Arissa needed Nathan's help to yank one of them open.

Inside was cooler than the outside air but still a bit hot, as if they didn't run their air conditioning unless it was necessary. The sounds of quiet conversations in Spanish filled the air. Arissa, being Filipino, almost looked like she could be Hispanic, but Nathan with his paler skin stuck out like a sore thumb.

"Let me talk, okay?" She ushered Charity into line.

He frowned. "Why?"

"Because you look like you're going to *arrest* someone."

The chagrined expression on his face made her smile, and suddenly it was as if they weren't on the run, as if the shooting hadn't happened, and he was simply running errands with her. As if things between them were normal and good.

They might one day be normal but they'd never be good. She told herself to get a grip just as the next teller called her over.

"My brother died and I want to access his account. This is his daughter and I'm her legal guardian." Arissa passed over the guardianship papers as well as her Los Angeles driver's license. "My address is the same as my brother's address in your database, and here's his account number." She'd copied the account number from the letter Mark had received onto a piece of paper, which she slid over to the teller. "I don't have his death certificate, but I have his social security number, and here's a printout of his obituary." Liam had thought of that, and searched the newspaper online archives until he found it. She also passed over Charity's identification card and a photocopy of her birth certificate.

A more vigilant bank would probably require the death certificate as well as the results of the DNA test she'd had done, but luckily, First Sonoma didn't ask many questions. The teller did scrutinize the papers, but quickly nodded and searched through her computer, an ancient machine that whirred so loudly Arissa hoped her request wasn't going to cause it to crash. The teller finally said, "I have his information here."

"I'd like his account statements, please." She wondered if he had years and years of records, and envisioned more papers to pore through. "I also want access to his safe deposit box."

"He opted to have his account statements online," the teller said.

Arissa was surprised the bank was that technologically advanced, but then again, if their patrons had access to the internet, it was less costly to the bank to give electronic statements rather than paper ones. "I don't have his password."

"Here, I'll write it down." The teller gave her a piece of paper with the same password Mark had used for his email account. "Do you have his safe deposit key?"

Arissa's heart sank. "No. It might be with his things, but I couldn't find it."

"I can get you another key, but it'll take two or three weeks."

Weeks? Could they stay with Liam that long? Would the LSL gang find them by then? "All right," she said slowly.

"Could I have a telephone number?"

Before she could answer, Nathan suddenly rattled off a phone number to the teller. "Liam's home phone," he told Arissa.

Right. Because in a couple weeks, she wouldn't be sure she'd still be using the burner cell phone he'd given to her.

They left the bank and had driven about a mile or two away, passing the local hardware store. Migrant workers often congregated at the corner of the parking lot, an unofficial place for building contractors and ranch foremen to stop and pick up extra help for the day. Arissa was idly looking at the sun-browned men. Two better-dressed men were talking to a handful of them—probably contractors looking for help.

One of those contractors turned to look at Nathan's car as they slowed in traffic.

It was one of the Filipino men from the rest stop.

Arissa yelped before she could help herself. The man recognized her immediately and yelled to his partner. The two of them dashed to a black BMW SUV parked a few feet away from the congregation of migrant workers.

"Nathan!"

"I see them." He yanked on the steering wheel and swerved around the car in front of him, jamming on the accelerator.

This time, they were in Nathan's SUV and not Malaya's aunt's beat-up car, but the BMW SUV had a more powerful engine and soon caught up with them on the smooth Sonoma roads. Arissa caught sight of the black vehicle, its chrome glinting in the sunlight, a couple cars behind them. "Do you see them?" she asked him.

"Yes."

"How are you going to shake them?" All she could see on either side were vineyards, since they were on the outskirts of Sonoma. Vineyards and gently curving roads, without many side roads to turn on. Even if they did turn right or left, it would be easy for the BMW to spot them in the flat fields.

But to her surprise, Nathan smiled grimly. "They're in *my* backyard, now."

He zoomed down the road, away from Sonoma and Liam and First Sonoma Bank. There was plenty of traffic since the vineyards were opening for wine tasting, so he often had to pause behind cars pulling right or left into vineyard driveways. He passed a lumbering truck filled with bright oranges, and the BMW followed easily.

Arissa's only consolation was that the driving had put Charity to sleep in her car seat. Thank goodness she usually fell asleep in cars no matter what time of day.

Nathan took them through winding roads that meandered through the foothills until

Arissa didn't know which direction they were headed. "Where are you going?"

"Santa Rosa."

"Why there?"

"It's a town with more urban streets."

Just when she thought the winding road was going to make her sick, they passed a golf course and suddenly they left the fields and entered a town. In fact, it looked a lot like some of the suburban sections of Los Angeles.

But it also allowed the BMW to gain on them until they were right on their tail.

"Are they going to ram us or something? What are they going to do?"

"I got the feeling they didn't expect to see us." Nathan cut around a few cars, but the pursuers followed. "They lost any element of surprise."

Arissa glanced at the gas tank, which was three-quarters full. "Are they hoping they have more gas than we do?"

"They could be waiting for us to do something stupid so they can grab you. Or they're hoping for an opportunity to force us to stop."

Arissa looked back. "Nathan, one of them is on his cell phone." Who was he calling? Did they have more gang members up here in Sonoma? Could they call reinforcements?

"That's too bad."

"Huh?"

"It's too bad he's talking to his gang, because they're about to lose us."

They were driving on a busy street with two lanes in either direction, separated by a double yellow line. Nathan abruptly twisted the wheel and swerved in a left turn directly in front of an oncoming wave of cars.

Arissa's heart choked her throat as a lime-green pickup truck grew large in her vision, as the sound of squealing tires filled her ears. She slammed her hand against the dashboard to brace herself, digging her nails into the hard contours. She didn't have time or breath to scream.

Then they were zooming down a side street, car horns blaring behind them. She twisted and saw the BMW trying to brake to follow them, but instead it overshot the side street, nearly colliding with the cars behind them.

Nathan turned left down another street, then he twisted their way through the streets of Santa Rosa until he got onto a freeway on-ramp. "Keep watch, see if they're following."

Arissa scanned the cars behind them, but there were few cars on the freeway and it was easy to see that the BMW wasn't there. She kept watch for several miles while Nathan headed back to Liam's place. He took smaller streets there, avoiding heavy traffic roads. The BMW never reappeared. Remembering that one of the men had made a phone call, she also checked to make sure they weren't being followed by any other cars—she kept tabs on which cars were behind them, but none of them followed for very long, and none of them reappeared.

There were absolutely no cars behind them when Nathan finally turned into the short street that led to Liam's duplex but she didn't breathe freely until they had parked the car.

She bowed her head and sagged against

her seat belt. They'd escaped those men again. *Thank You, Lord.*

"Arissa." Nathan's voice was quiet in the silent car.

She looked at him.

His eyes were a silver-green sea that she drowned in, warm and comforting. "Are you okay?"

She managed to nod. "It was a shock to see them again. Your driving was great."

"I'm sorry if I scared you."

"You didn't scare me, I trust you." The words were out of her mouth before she could think.

He seemed uncomfortable, and she didn't understand why she'd said it. But it was true—she did trust him. She knew he'd take care of them, at least as long as they were here in Sonoma.

She reached out and touched his face, cupping his cheek. His skin was cool but warmed beneath her fingers.

He tensed under her touch for a brief moment, but then he raised his hand to fold over hers.

That point of contact wasn't a lightning bolt, or a spark, or a sizzle. It was a glowing warmth that started in her hand and rolled down her arm like honey.

He closed his eyes briefly and turned his face into her palm. His lips were a hair's breadth away from her skin.

Then Charity woke and let out a fussy cry. "Aunt Rissa."

Arissa blinked as if waking from a dream. As she pulled away her hand, she thought his fingers might have tightened for a brief moment—but he still let her go.

She and Nathan were silent as they entered Liam's home. She preferred it that way. Why had she touched him? Why was she fooling herself into thinking anything could come of this? He might care about her to some extent, maybe because of the past, but he had obviously been uncomfortable with her trust, so there was even less of a chance he'd want to deepen their relationship on any level. Anyway, she shouldn't even be considering this while she was on the run from gang members.

Liam looked up from his computer as they walked in and saw their faces. "What happened?"

But before they could answer, Charity asked, "Aunt Rissa, can I play outside?"

Arissa wasn't sure Liam even had a backyard, and she didn't want Charity wandering in the next-door vineyard, since she wasn't sure it was snake-free.

"I'll take her," Nathan suddenly said. "You fill in Liam."

"No, I can go for a short walk with her."

But Nathan shook his head. "I need to stretch my leg."

His eyes caught hers, and her next protest died on her lips. He could take away her breath with just a look. She marveled at it even as she mentally kicked herself for reacting to him this way.

"Come on, *nene*." The Filipino endearment rolled naturally from his lips, and Charity responded by taking the hand he held out.

Liam stood and stretched, his arm moving stiffly. "Let's all go outside. I've been working the entire time you've been gone."

Arissa discovered that while Liam didn't have a backyard, his back door opened into a dirt track, parallel to the driveway in front of the line of duplexes. On one side of the dirt road were the houses, but on the other side stood the large field of grapevines. The dirt track led up beside the rows of grapevines to a small grassy area, and then the rolling foothill, dotted with two lone trees. Arissa and Liam walked behind Nathan, who matched Charity's slow steps.

"We saw the two men who shot at us at the rest stop," Arissa said.

Liam's eyes darkened to indigo. "At the bank?"

"No, thank goodness. We'd left the bank, but we saw them outside the hardware store, talking to some of the migrant workers."

"So they were in Sonoma? Looking for you?"

"I guess."

Nathan glanced back at them. "Not necessarily. But they know you're near Sonoma now."

"It seems coincidental they'd be in So-noma, right after shooting at you."

"But if they did know I was in Sonoma, how'd they find out?" Arissa said.

"Look." Charity stopped and squatted in front of a patch of bright yellow flowers growing along the side of the path.

Nathan turned to Arissa. "If they were tracking your friend's cell phone—the one she left in her car—from the time you were parked in front of my parents' house, they'll have known you stopped in Sonoma for a while. And since I'm with you, they might figure that I'd keep you nearby since I'm from here."

"Maybe we should leave Sonoma."

"We will, but I think we're safe with Liam for now." Nathan glanced at Charity. "I've thought of other places, but they wouldn't be easy with a child."

"Uncle Nathan, let's run!" Charity grabbed his hand and started pumping her little legs.

A smile lit his face, making him seem a decade younger, and he pretended to run alongside her.

"Do you think they know about the bank?" Liam asked.

"I don't think so. There are any number of places we could have been before they saw us. And they have no reason to suspect that Mark had any particular ties to Sonoma— we're the only ones who know he actually had a bank account up here." She watched Charity chatting with Nathan. "The Fischers mentioned they'd seen Mark a few times around here, but he said he was visiting our aunt. It never even occurred to me he'd have something like a hidden bank account." That reminded her, she wanted to call her parents from a safe phone to make sure they were okay and also to ask if Aunt Luellen had ever mentioned Mark visiting her. "When we get back to the house, I need to access Mark's bank statements online."

"I looked through the boxes after you left," Liam said. "There was nothing else from Sonoma. I even skimmed through some of his credit card statements, and he never charged anything up here. If that one let-ter is the only clue about his ties to Sonoma then that means he went through a lot of effort to hide it."

"What else does he have up here? A storage unit? A post office box?"

Liam shrugged. "He could have all those things, but there's no way to know."

His words hung in the warm air. How could the sun be so bright, the fields be so verdant, when inside she felt so cold? Bees buzzed around some wild roses growing at the end of one of the rows of grapevines, and butterflies flitted across their path, alighting on patches of wildflowers. They mocked her because her life was dark like a moldy wood.

Ahead of her, Charity raced toward the grassy patch at the base of the foothill, but she saw Nathan's leg trembling with the strain as the path began to climb. Yet when he reached Charity, he still laughed with her and obligingly spun her in a pirouette when she ordered him to, despite the pain tightening the skin at his eyes.

She approached him and tried to smile for Charity's sake. "Can I call my parents? I want to make sure they're okay."

He nodded and handed her his prepaid cell phone.

She was fairly certain the gang would never make the connection between herself and her discipler, but she did worry about how dangerous it was that her folks were still in Los Angeles.

She dialed. "Hi, Mrs. Fuchikami, it's Arissa."

"How are you doing, dear?"

"We're fine."

"I've been praying for you."

Her voice felt hollow as she answered, "Thank you, I appreciate your prayers."

At her words, Nathan turned away and began talking to Charity about the wildflowers she was picking and mangling. His reaction made her sad but unsure what she could do. Had he stopped praying altogether?

"Let me get your parents," Mrs. Fuchikami said, and soon her mother was on the line.

"Arissa, are you all right? We're so worried."

"We're fine, Mom. How are you guys doing?"

"Your dad's going crazy, but I just remind him you didn't escape kidnappers for nothing and he should make sure he doesn't get you in more trouble."

Arissa couldn't help smiling at her mother's way of putting things. But she also had to keep this conversation short so she got to the point. "Mom, when you talk to Aunt Luellen, did she ever mention Mark visiting her in Sonoma by himself in the months before he died?"

Nathan turned to look at her with eyebrows raised.

"What?" Mom said in surprise. "No. Mark never went to see her by himself. And you know your aunt Luellen would have made sure to tell me if he had."

"Oh, okay." She had expected that answer, but it still disappointed her. She gave Nathan a slight shake of her head. She had begun to realize that Mark had probably lied about going to see Aunt Luellen, but a part of her had hoped that in addition to his clandestine activities in Sonoma, Mark had indeed paid

Aunt Luellen a visit. She might have found out something about why he'd been here.

"Arissa, I know you said not to, but your father checked his email."

"Oh, Mom…"

"Wait, listen to me." There was a strain in her mother's voice that made her stomach cramp. "Aunt Desiree heard something. Your friend Malaya is missing."

She wanted to gasp but bit her lip, trying not to react so she wouldn't alarm Charity.

"Aunt Desiree heard it from Malaya's neighbors. Her coworker came by her parents' house because Malaya missed her shift at work, but Malaya's parents are out of town right now. No one can report her missing to the police since she's an adult and hasn't been gone for very long, but everyone's worried because she never misses work."

It was true. Malaya was extremely responsible and a little obsessive-compulsive, so missing work was a clear sign something was wrong.

Missing! Because of Arissa? How could she have involved Malaya in all this? Arissa took deep breaths, trying not to be sick all over the grass at the side of the path. She focused on Nathan, who had knelt in front of Charity. His body shielded the little girl from seeing Arissa. She wondered if he had done that on purpose.

"That'll make a nice bouquet." He gestured to the wilted flowers clutched in her tiny hands.

"This is for you." Charity handed Nathan a blue flower.

"Thank you. How's this?" He tucked it behind his ear, and Charity giggled.

"Arissa?" her mother said in the phone.

"Oh, Mom." Arissa gave a broken sob, then she took a deep breath. "Don't let anyone know where you are, all right?"

"We won't. We promise."

"I love you. Bye." She turned, putting her hand to her mouth. She had to stay strong. For Charity.

"Arissa," Nathan said in a low, calm voice.

She pivoted around. Nathan still crouched with Charity, but watched her with a steady gaze. Liam stood a few feet away, looking anxious.

She took another deep breath, which seemed to help her pull herself together. Then she spoke. "My friend Malaya..."

"The one who lent you her car."

She nodded. Swallowed. "Mom said that she's gone missing."

And it was all her fault.

SEVEN

Arissa sat on the edge of the mattress as Charity sleepily sang to the doll resting on the pillow next to her. She stroked the girl's soft hair with hands that shook because of the weight of guilt crushing her breastbone.

She didn't want to move from this spot, from the comfort of sitting next to Charity. She didn't want to return to the real world and the danger she had to face—the emotions she had to suppress.

But she couldn't let this news about Malaya paralyze her. There was too much she had to do. She had to keep them safe, without putting anyone else in danger.

She rose to her feet, swaying a moment and taking a deep breath to steady her knees, then walked out of the bedroom.

The smell of butter hitting a hot skillet followed by simmering tomatoes wafted into her as soon as she entered the living room. Nathan stood at the stove stirring something in a small pot, and she saw a frying pan with a sandwich grilling on the other burner. He turned to her. "Since you made Charity a grilled cheese sandwich, I thought I'd make some for us, too. With tomato soup. Sound good?"

The simple act of eating lunch eased the tightness in her shoulder blades. "Great." She'd felt too stressed to be hungry when making Charity's sandwich, but now her stomach grumbled.

She helped Liam clear the small table of his paperwork, setting the laptop safely in a corner. Liam eyed her. "You okay?" he asked softly.

She nodded, not trusting her voice.

They squeezed onto the small table with their plates and bowls, and Arissa hesitated. "May I say grace?" she asked.

Liam nodded, not surprised by her request. Perhaps he was Christian, or from a Christian family.

But Nathan's jaw tensed for a brief moment, and he looked away. Then he relaxed with a visible effort and said curtly, "Sure."

But even as she said a prayer, Arissa felt uncomfortable, as if the words just hit the ceiling and bounced back. Her heart was cold inside her, a strange feeling in the year since she'd become a Christian. She'd gotten used to that quiet peace that touched her whenever she prayed, but now her prayers seemed rote, dull, lifeless.

She also realized this was the first time she'd prayed in a while. When had she last spent time with God?

What was there to say to Him besides a fervent plea to survive? And what good would that do? What she needed was answers or a really juicy lead on what Mark had been doing, and it wasn't as if God could deliver those things in her lap right at this moment.

She ended the short prayer a bit awkwardly, and they started eating in silence. She normally loved melting grilled cheese, but something about the prayer unsettled her, and the sandwich tasted too salty and too oily in her mouth, the soup too sweet.

Finally Nathan cleared his throat. "We need to figure out what to do now."

Arissa wiped her mouth with her napkin. "I have Mark's password, so I can review his bank statements. Do you mind lending me your computer again?" she asked Liam.

"Go ahead."

"I can look through Mark's boxes again for that safe deposit key." Nathan threw his napkin on his empty plate. "Now that I know what to search for, maybe I can figure out if he hid it inside something innocuous."

Privately Arissa thought that Internal Affairs would have found it if it were there, but she knew Nathan felt helpless and restless, not knowing what he could do besides laying low here at Liam's house.

"If you don't mind, I have calls I need to make." Liam stood with his plate. "I'll use the phone next door so I don't disturb you two."

"I'm sorry for forcing you out of your own house."

He only shook his head and grinned. "I get fed in return—I'm fine with it."

She helped Nathan clean up the dishes, then got onto the internet on Liam's laptop. She logged into the bank's online website using Mark's account number and password.

The amount in his account made her gasp.

"What's wrong?" Nathan was at her side in an instant, enveloping her in musk and lime that seemed to calm her as she struggled to draw in breath.

He stiffened as he saw the amount of money Mark had saved. "When did he start depositing funds?"

She searched the records and found the account was about five years old. "His first deposit was a few months after Mom's cancer diagnosis."

According to the electronic records, he had deposited large amounts of cash at the bank's ATM at irregular intervals. "Are these..." She swallowed, then pointed to the screen. "Are these deposit dates about the same as dates when the LAPD..."

"There were several cases and operations

where information was given to the drug dealers before the LAPD arrived. I don't know those dates offhand. I'd have to talk to my friend Steve to ask him to look them up for me."

There was a chance these cash deposits weren't because Mark had been paid off by the drug cartel. Maybe he got this cash selling stuff on eBay or something. Arissa drew in a breath, but it sounded to her ears like a sob.

The next thing she noticed about the account was that the only withdrawals were in the form of checks—no cash withdrawals at the ATM or from the bank tellers. The bank had scanned images of the checks online, so she clicked on a link and a pop-up window appeared. It took a few seconds for the image of the check—back and front— to appear, but she recognized the recipient. "He paid off Mom's medical bills."

She clicked on more checks, one after another. They all paid for her mother's health-care charges, to a variety of places. "Dad never said anything about Mark paying the bills for him."

"He could have intercepted the statements when they arrived in the mail—you two were living with your parents at the time, so it would have been easy to do."

She nodded, tears starting to pool in her eyes. In the first few months, he'd used all his money to pay Mom's bills. His account balance had remained low. Then he started making more deposits and although he also paid off more of Mom's charges, the amount he deposited exceeded the checks he was writing.

"How did he get this money?" Her voice had a slightly hysterical edge to it.

"Arissa." Nathan put his hand on her shoulder and forced her to angle toward him. His eyes were close to hers, dark gray and velvety. "Whatever he was doing to get this money, he only did it for one reason—to help your mother. That's the Mark I remember."

Nathan's voice shook slightly. Perhaps this new knowledge about his partner had affected him—for so long, all he'd known was what he'd seen, Mark selling out the LAPD. But here was proof about why he did it—a son's devotion to his sick mother.

It still didn't excuse what he did. Arissa understood that. But images began to flash in front of her eyes—Mark cradling Mom's fragile form after they'd heard about the diagnosis, tears shining in his eyes even as he reassured her she'd be all right. Mark bending down to tenderly kiss Mom's cheek as she lay in the hospital bed. Mark cooking and cleaning for Mom even though he'd come off a long shift. Mark holding Mom's hand as she slept, the chemo making her weak and sick.

Yes, Mark would have committed any felony to save their mother, without hesitation or regret.

His last check had posted after his death, but had been written the day before the shoot-out at the chop shop, a payment for some tests Mom had had done. Arissa reached out to touch the laptop screen, tracing his signature on the check, just barely readable from the scanned .jpg file.

There was nothing else in his account but those cash deposits and checks. She checked other tabs on the website, but he hadn't taken out any loans—obviously—and he hadn't set up any automatic bill payments.

But then she had an idea. She clicked on his account information and found the link to update his settings. There, a Yahoo! email account she had never seen before. He'd had his account statements emailed to him there.

Nathan stared at the computer. "Internal Affairs checked his computer at work—and I'm assuming they checked his home computer, too. If they'd found this email address, they'd have checked it and discovered this bank account."

"He must have gone through extreme measures not to check this email account on any computer that would leave a record in the browser history." Arissa opened a new window and opened Yahoo.com, then selected "Check Mail." She typed in the email address, hesitated, then typed in the password he'd used for his other personal email and the same password he'd used for this bank account.

She successfully logged in.

The emails she read made her want to scream.

Some were obviously from members of the LSLs because they signed their unique nicknames, which Nathan could recognize. Other nicknames were not so obvious— he got several emails from "Sleepy" and "Grumpy" and Nathan remarked that practically every gang in Los Angeles had members with nicknames like the seven dwarfs.

But the content of the emails were similar, and they all pointed to one indisputable fact—Mark was selling information from the LAPD.

Her eyes burned as she read email after email, but she couldn't stop, she couldn't turn herself away. She couldn't end the torture.

Finally Nathan grabbed her hand as it worked the mouse and forced her to let it go. "Arissa, we don't need to read any more."

"Yes, I do," she bit out, although now her

throat was burning and acidic tears scalded her cheeks as they fell.

"Arissa—"

"I need to see everything. I need to know everything he did."

"You do know—"

"I don't know how he could do this." She clamped her teeth together, felt them scrape against each other.

"Yes." His firm fingers grasped her chin, turning her away from the computer to look into his eyes. "You do."

And suddenly she was sobbing and wailing, and Nathan held her close, her cries muffled by his shoulder.

For so long, she had believed Mark was innocent. Even when the gang had kidnapped her, she had never quite relinquished the hope that it was some misunderstanding.

But here was proof. Horrible, finger-pointing proof that her brother wasn't the upstanding police officer he'd presented to her parents and to their family, but a filthy, dirty mole. Her brother, who had nagged her in her earlier years about her partying and drinking. Her brother, who hadn't wanted their father to go to the unsavory money lenders when the bills started coming in.

What ludicrous hypocrisy.

She screamed into Nathan's shirt, twisting it in her fists. She thought she might have even pounded his chest with her hands a few times in her frustration, her rage, her sorrow.

He held her, a steady rock, and his hand never stopped smoothing her head.

Finally her emotions rolled back, like a receding ocean wave. She felt drained but strangely calm as she tried to pull away from him, but Nathan resisted and held her close. He reached out and grabbed some clean paper napkins from their lunch, handing them to her. She wiped her nose and face even as she remained leaning against his chest, her other arm wrapped around his waist and gripping the back of his shirt. His arms around her tightened, a reassurance that warmed her even more than the heat from his body against her cheek.

Then she backed away slightly, reached up and pulled his head down to kiss him.

She felt his start of surprise, but almost immediately his lips warmed and softened against hers. She hadn't thought his arms could tighten around her any more, but they did, holding her close as if he could shield her from a nuclear bomb.

And that's what his kiss was like. Maybe because she trusted him so completely. Maybe because of remnants of the past and her attraction to the tall, mischievous narcotics detective her brother had introduced to the family. Maybe because he had held her in her pain, setting himself aside to comfort her when she knew this proof about Mark must devastate him, too.

Nathan was so many things—the adventurous man he'd been, the determined man he was now. He'd been shadowed by his pain and disappointment but was still true to his inner values, his identity as a protector, first and foremost. He made her want to drop the defensive walls around her heart and embrace all of him, his pain and his joy, his weakness and his strengths. She no longer saw him as the idealized detective she'd known three years ago, but a man whose honorable heart shone brighter than the noonday sun.

But even as he deepened the kiss, she knew that this moment only highlighted the fact that their relationship could never go beyond this point. Her brother had been a mole, the mole who had cut Nathan's career short. She and Charity were in danger and may need to run so they wouldn't put anyone else at risk, including his parents. And what kind of man saddled himself with a woman with a three-year-old, much less one with a drug gang after her?

She still reveled in his closeness, in the touch of his hand at her jaw, the scent of musk that wrapped around her. And another tear fell from her eye, this one because these sensations were everything she'd never have again.

"Arissa, don't cry." He drew back his head and his thumb wiped away the tear.

She looked up at his wonderful, handsome face, and her heart shattered. This could never be. "You were right," she whispered brokenly.

His eyes faltered, and their connection dissolved.

She sat back in her chair, licked her lips nervously and tasted him there. She closed her eyes for a moment, clinging to the last threads of warmth she had felt in his arms.

Then she opened her eyes and straightened her back. Time to face reality. Her brother had been a mole.

In the silence, her eyes had been staring at the computer screen, but unseeing. Now, however, she focused on a folder in his email account labeled "Jemma." Mark's girlfriend, Charity's mother. She reached for the mouse and clicked on the folder.

Hundreds of letters, some teasing, some a bit mundane, some racy and heated, some unbearably tender. Mark had truly loved Jemma and had been excited about the child she carried.

From what Arissa could infer from them, Jemma's father had known, and although he'd been worried about the fact Mark was a cop, he hadn't disapproved. Since Jemma's parents knew, she hadn't been pressured by anyone else to divulge the identity of her lover. The rest of her extended family respected the silence of her parents as to the father of her child.

"Mark met her because..." Arissa swallowed.

"Because he'd been meeting the members of the gang," Nathan said, which was kinder phrasing than, *because he'd been selling information.*

She turned to him, capturing his whole attention with the earnestness in her eyes. "Tell me what happened that day at the chop shop. Tell me what you saw."

He looked away, and for a few moments she thought he'd refuse her, but then he said, "It started at the station. I saw a green folder on his desk. He wasn't sitting there at the moment, and I don't know why, but I looked inside. It was information about a sting operation planned for the next morning."

He sighed. "I thought it was a bit unusual that he had the info, but I figured maybe the captain in charge of the raid had asked Mark for some help. I went back to my desk. But then Mark came to his desk and said he was heading home a little early. He laid his jacket on the folder, and then picked it up as he left."

"That's why you followed him that day."

"I almost didn't find him because he was driving your car instead of his. Finally I recognized the paint chip pattern on your trunk because it looks like a bird. I followed him to the chop shop, parked a couple blocks away and snuck inside. I hid behind a blue Buick. I saw Mark hand the folder to Johnny Capuno. Johnny was about to hand Mark an envelope—and even from where I was hidden I could see it was gaping open, full of cash—when I heard a shout behind me, and a bullet hit the Buick only a few inches away from my shoulder."

His hand rubbed his thigh, although Arissa didn't think he realized he was doing it. "It was chaotic. I hid behind a nearby Trans Am and returned fire. I saw Johnny darting out of the chop shop with the folder in one hand and the envelope of money still in the other."

"That's why the information and the money was never found on Mark's body," Arissa said slowly.

"There were LSL gang members everywhere, and while some were shooting at me, I think most were confused. They didn't understand who was the threat."

Arissa thought back to the report she'd seen of the shoot-out. "The forensics report said several gang members were shot by guns belonging to their own crew."

"It seemed like there were bullets flying everywhere. Then I saw Mark take cover behind a Lexus." Nathan's face paled as he remembered. "He…he saw me behind the Trans Am. And then…" He suddenly grimaced and turned away from her, his hand bunched up in a fist.

"Nathan." She touched his fist, then smoothed fingers over his cheek. "Please tell me." A part of her wondered if maybe he needed to let it out, if making him talk about this was cathartic somehow. She wondered if he'd gone to a counselor at all.

He finally turned to her with a face tense and hard. "Mark saw me, raised his gun and shot at me."

She felt as if she'd been shot herself. Pain blossomed at the base of her throat, making it hard to breathe. She forced herself to swallow. "He's the one who…your leg? But I thought…"

"No, he missed me. But I'll never forget his face when he fired. He looked absolutely determined."

Arissa couldn't think of anything to say.

Nathan continued, "I raised my gun—it was almost automatic. But I didn't fire. I couldn't."

"Oh, Nathan," she whispered.

"Then a gang member ran into view and shot at me. I returned fire and ran behind a Taurus. I remembered hearing the sirens at that point, but as soon as I got behind the car, I…" He winced. "I got hit."

His femur bone shattered by a gang member's bullet.

"I don't remember much after that."

Arissa's mind turned back to the police report she'd pored over, had almost memorized. "Nathan, you were behind a Trans Am when Mark shot at you?"

He blinked at her. "Yeah."

She remembered something from the police report, something she'd noticed only because it had involved Mark. "There was a gang member found dead behind a Trans Am, directly in line of sight from where Mark's body was found." She didn't know why, but she grabbed Nathan's hand. "He'd been shot with Mark's gun."

His fingers twitched beneath hers. He was silent a minute or two. "Are you sure? How do you know?"

"I got a copy of the police report and I went over it, even though the IA investigation was closed by then. I made note of everything involving Mark—including his gun. He shot three gang members, counting the one behind a Trans Am."

Nathan pulled his hand from hers and stood, pacing in the small living room space, his palm rubbing his forehead. "No one else shot with Mark's gun, it was found in his hand." He looked at her with eyes like burning coals. "You're saying he shot at a gang member who was behind me."

"I don't know. The report doesn't say when he shot the man. It could have been after you hid behind the Taurus."

"But the man was behind the Trans Am?"

"Yes. I don't know exactly where you were positioned behind the Trans Am—"

"There was only one spot shielding me from the gang members, and that was behind the rear bumper. The gang members were mostly near the front of the shop."

"Mark shot the man near the back left side of the car. The report said he was hit on the dead center of his heart."

Nathan's movements became quicker, more jerky. "I don't remember seeing anyone. But it could be I just didn't notice."

She wet her lips. "So it's possible Mark shot in your direction because he was aiming for the gang member behind you."

Nathan stopped pacing, and in a voice she

could barely hear, he breathed, "He saved my life."

The silence between them stretched taut. Nathan stood looking blindly out the living room window. She wished he'd sit down, she wasn't sure how his leg felt after his pacing.

He abruptly turned to her, eyes burning again. "We have to find that safe deposit key. We can't afford to wait three weeks."

His shift in emotions startled her, but only briefly. "Internal Affairs didn't find it," she stated.

"So it wouldn't be in any of his things. But it would have to be somewhere he could access it easily."

"The storage unit?"

"Where in the storage unit?" he asked.

She cast her mind over all the furniture and boxes. "It could be anywhere."

"No, if it's true that your family shares that unit, he'd have put it somewhere none of your family members would stumble over it."

He had a point. "Everything that was his we turned over to IA. There's nothing in that storage unit that they haven't seen except that shoe box of mail that came after IA took everything."

"Would he have hidden the key in something belonging to your parents?"

"If he did and Dad or Mom found it, they would have asked him about it."

"Mark would have wanted to avoid that." Nathan went back to rubbing his palm over his broad forehead, deep in thought. "Where would I hide a key?"

In something IA hadn't seen…someplace the family wouldn't accidentally stumble over it… "Maybe it *wasn't* hidden," she said slowly.

"What do you mean?"

"Maybe it was in plain sight." Had he really hidden it there? "Two or three Sundays a month, our extended family would gather at Aunt Chichi's house for potluck dinner. As long as I can remember, she's had a glass fishbowl on the hallway table filled with orphaned keys that belonged to unknown locks. Not just her family's keys—the rest of us started throwing our mystery keys in there, too."

"I agree it would be a good hiding place, but what makes you think Mark would put his key there?"

"Once, I had to leave the dinner because I had to get up early for work the next morning, but Mark hid my car key in the bowl. It took me forever to find it because it was buried under the other keys." She smiled remembering his figure, doubled up with laughter as she tore through the house, up-ending couch cushions and threatening to kill him. "When I finally found them, he said that the bowl was the perfect place to hide keys."

Nathan frowned slightly. "But the bowl of keys is in your aunt's house, not yours. So he'd have to go to her house to get his safe deposit key."

"But we had dinner at her house several times a month because she had room for all of us. It's a family thing—we're always gathering to eat."

"Would the gang know she's your aunt? Would they talk to her or—"

"Aunt Chichi died a year after Mark's death. All her things, including the key bowl, were stuck in storage."

Light dawned in his eyes. "In your aunt Desiree's storage unit. Since it's registered under her name, no one but family members know you're sharing the unit."

Arissa shrugged. "One of my ex-boyfriends knew, because he went with me to the storage unit once when I needed to get some filed papers for our taxes, but according to Facebook, he's in Singapore now."

Nathan studied her for a long moment. "How are you feeling?"

"What?"

"Are you up for traveling to Los Angeles right now? Would Charity be able to sleep in the car?"

"Now?" She looked at the clock, which said three in the afternoon. "We'll be in L.A. around ten o'clock at night."

"It's a twenty-four-hour-access storage facility. I remember seeing that the last time we went."

"But where would we stay for the night in L.A.?"

"We'd drive back here. We can get back before dawn."

"Are you really willing to stay up so long and drive?" She didn't want to mention his leg, but she was also worried about how he was holding up under these extended hours and constant strain.

He looked at her with a long-suffering expression, as if he knew what she was thinking. "I'll be fine, *Mom*."

"Why not wait until tomorrow morning?"

"Because." He stopped pacing and stood in front of her, his hands on her shoulders. "I think the answer to why the gang is after you is in that safe deposit box."

EIGHT

It had been a long drive, but the urgency sizzling in Nathan's gut kept him alert. He'd called in sick to work today, and he didn't need to go in tomorrow, but he still wanted answers sooner than later. And if he had to trek to Los Angeles and back twice in two days, then that's what he was willing to do.

Besides, he needed to *do* something, or his thoughts would overwhelm him. Arissa's observation about the gang member behind the Trans Am had shaken him badly. He'd seen Mark's face and the gun pointing at him so often in his nightmares that it felt like the image had imprinted on the back of his eyelids.

Mark had looked determined. Not angry, not guilty, not reckless. Then he'd fired—

and possibly shot a gang member to save Nathan's life.

Nathan tried to remember now what Mark had looked like when Nathan pointed his own gun at his partner. Had he been surprised? Accepting? Resentful? Nathan simply couldn't remember.

He had always known that not shooting Mark had been the right thing to do. A gang member's bullet had hit Mark in the leg, severing his femoral artery so that he bled to death while Nathan lay a few yards away, nearly wild with pain from his shattered thigh.

Somehow knowing that Mark might have saved his life made Nathan's feelings about that day more complicated. Mark was a mole. Mark was his partner. Mark sold out his fellow cops. Mark protected him.

His friend's sister sat a few inches away, her body twisted around as she spoke to Charity in the backseat, but she might as well be miles away from him. He had held her and comforted her not just because she needed someone, but also because *he* wanted to be the one there for her. Yet he'd been able to maintain control over his feelings—until she'd kissed him.

Her kiss had surprised him, and he hadn't been able to resist her, but when he'd felt her cheek wet with that tear, something inside him jolted back to reality.

She deserved better than a broken man. He'd never be able to carry her over a threshold. He'd never be able to run with Charity. He still woke up shouting from the nightmares.

He was too wounded physically and emotionally to give her what she would need.

He maneuvered through the traffic of L.A., busy even this late at night. As he neared the storage facility, he kept his eyes open for any surveillance—cars with men waiting inside, ominous vans parked alongside the street. He didn't see anything.

Arissa took out the prepaid cell phone he'd given to her. "I know what will help." She dialed. "Hi, Tito, it's Arissa…We're fine. Have you heard anything? No? Good. I'm calling about Aunt Chichi's key bowl, remember that? You and your mom were the ones who packed Aunty's house when she died. Do you remember where you stowed it?"

He couldn't see her face very clearly in the darkness, except for when a passing streetlamp flickered onto her, but he could see the confused tilt of her head.

"Say that again?" Arissa nodded slowly, but not very confidently. "Well, maybe I'll just look through the boxes in that corner and I'll get lucky.... No, I don't want you to come to the unit if you're busy.... Well, if you're sure..." She said goodbye and disconnected the call. "My cousin Tito said he'd meet us at the storage unit in twenty minutes to help us find the key bowl. He wasn't entirely sure where his mom put it when they packed up Aunty Chichi's house."

Nathan turned into the driveway for the storage facility. "Maybe we'll find it before he gets here."

The facility was dark despite the floodlights spaced out in intervals along the walls of the units. Nathan parked where he had before and Arissa carried a sleeping Charity toward the building where her aunt's storage unit was. They crossed under a few floodlights to get to the door, which he opened with her storage unit key. As he fumbled with the door lock, a car engine nearby suddenly came to life.

Nathan's body tensed as if an electrical current had zinged through it, but the small Honda Accord immediately drove away from them, heading out of the facility to the sound of a stereo system blasting some hip-hop music with overly loud bass beats.

Nathan got the door unlocked and they headed inside toward Arissa's family's storage unit.

The building seemed eerier in the darkness, although since there were no windows it shouldn't look any different from when they had visited during the day. He unlocked the storage unit door and turned on the lights.

"Tito said that Aunt Chichi's boxes are near my parents' in the far corner." Arissa nodded toward the back of the storage unit.

"I wonder if the dolls I took for Charity last time were from her house? They could have belonged to my cousin."

She lay Charity on a nearby couch and covered her with Nathan's jacket. Then the two of them started looking through the designated boxes.

They sifted briefly through some filled with clothes, but since Arissa knew the key bowl, filled with keys, would take up a large space and be very heavy, they didn't spend too much time on those boxes. Nathan thought they'd found it when he dragged out an extremely heavy one, but it ended up being full of her aunt's late husband's power tools.

They looked inside a box that appeared to be full of desk accessories, and Arissa shook her head. Nathan was about to move it when he noticed how heavy it was—more than he'd expect for a box with staplers, pens and a broken desk clock. He began pawing through it.

There. Hidden under a blotter that had been thrown on top was a heavy glass fishbowl. There were other things inside it—tennis balls, paper clips, erasers and random things that had probably fallen inside—but the edges of various keys could be seen underneath.

"I can't believe you found it so fast." Arissa reached in and hefted out the fishbowl. She tossed the extraneous objects and began scooping handfuls of keys.

Nathan found an empty basket and they threw the rejects in there after selecting any for the distinctive shape of a safe deposit key. "How in the world would Mark have found his key in all this?" Nathan dropped into the plant holder some tiny keys that looked like they belonged to padlocks.

Arissa stopped and stared hard at the bowl. "You're right. It's like when he hid my car keys." She abandoned the handful of keys she held and instead started sifting through the keys left in the bowl, her hand diving deeper until it seemed to be searching the bottom. "Got it!" She pulled from the sea of keys a keychain with a small circular fob that had the name and logo of Arissa's airline. "So that's where that keychain went. But what's this for?"

She held up the keychain and separated the two keys on the metal circle. One was obviously a safe deposit key, but the other reminded Nathan of his house key. "It looks like a dead-bolt key or a doorknob key."

"Did he have an apartment in Sonoma too?" Arissa frowned at the key. "I'm surprised he was able to keep that from the gang."

"They don't do background checks. Even if he took out an apartment in his name—which I doubt he did, he probably paid cash—the gang wouldn't have investigated deep enough to find out."

"If he paid cash for an apartment, it's probably been rented out again by now when he didn't pay rent." Arissa sighed. "Anything he had in the apartment would have been tossed out."

"You're probably right."

Nathan suddenly noticed the sound in the distance of a deep, overly loud stereo bass. It sounded familiar to the Honda Accord that had driven out of the facility parking lot, even though it played a different song. But then the sound abruptly stopped.

He was being paranoid. Still, they should get out of here now. "I'll put these boxes back. You call your cousin to let him know." Nathan pocketed the key chain.

"Aunty Rissa?" Charity said sleepily from the couch. She opened her eyes and blinked in confusion and fear at the strange surroundings. Arissa went to her, soothing her.

As Nathan slid the last box into place on the stack, they suddenly heard the door to the storage unit open.

They were expecting her cousin, but now Nathan realized they should have made sure it was locked. Arissa froze, and Nathan strained to listen.

The door didn't open with the breezy sound of Tito walking into his family's storage unit. The careful click of the doorknob, the soft creak of the hinges, made Nathan's shoulders tense. He waved to Arissa to get Charity away from the couch and behind some stacks of boxes. He eased his gun out of his holster.

His senses expanded, and he heard the soft *swish* of a shoe on the concrete floor, trying hard to be silent. If it were Tito, he would have expected the man to call out to them, but this intruder said nothing.

Nathan crept behind a dresser so he could peek toward the door, but the intruder had slipped down another row of space between furniture and boxes and he couldn't see him. Where would he reappear? Nathan scanned the storage unit. They were trapped. If bullets started flying, someone was going to be hurt.

And if there was one intruder, there was guaranteed to be more outside the storage unit and stationed beside Nathan's car.

Adrenaline galloped through his body, dulling the ache in his thigh. He couldn't fail Arissa and Charity. He had to protect them.

He squinted in the shadows cast by the fluorescent lights above and saw movement through the legs of a chair upended on top of another one.

Nathan saw the dark eyes of the other man over the top of a file cabinet at the same moment he spotted Nathan. He fired just as Nathan ducked, and the sound of the shot in the enclosed space deafened him so that he almost didn't hear the bullet thunking into the wooden dresser.

Charity screamed and began to cry.

Then a *second* man's voice said something angrily in Filipino.

Nathan's hand tightened around his gun. Charity's crying would draw the men right to her—the gang members might shoot in the general direction and possibly hit someone.

But the man didn't shoot, maybe because of what the other man said to him. And Nathan remembered that they'd kidnapped Arissa before, meaning they needed her alive. Not riddled with bullet holes.

He searched but couldn't find the man who'd fired. He couldn't see the second man, either, but they would both be heading toward Arissa and Charity. Nathan holstered his gun, then eased himself around the dresser and scooted between two stacks of boxes. Since he knew where they were heading, he could circle around behind them and tackle at least one of them, hopefully take him out quickly before dealing with the second man.

He slipped around a ratty recliner and under a dining room table before spotting one man creeping toward the corner of a stack of boxes. Charity continued to cry although he heard Arissa trying to shush the girl. Then he heard a blip, indicating Arissa's cell phone had gotten a text message.

The man would be onto Arissa in a moment.

Nathan sprang at him.

They both crashed into a bookshelf filled with small boxes. The shelf tilted backward but didn't hit the floor because of the items behind it. The heavy boxes on the shelves grazed Nathan's limbs as they slipped sideways and fell, hampering him from getting more than a few punches to the man's torso.

The second man called out, but he was

some distance away. Nathan had to take this first guy out fast.

The Filipino man was stocky, a little taller than Mark had been, and a lot faster. His fist came out of nowhere and Nathan rolled with the punch to lessen the impact on his cheek, but pain still exploded in stars in front of his eyes. Nathan swung out blindly and his fist grazed some body part.

The man grabbed Nathan and rolled so that they were off the tilted bookshelf and on the floor, but he caught sight of Nathan's face… and then a smirk flashed over his mouth.

The man let go of Nathan's shirtfront and landed two hard, swift punches to his injured thigh.

The blows felt like a ton of bricks slamming into his bone in rapid succession. Nathan cried out, his body already twisted in pain, helpless. He tried to block out the pain, to get up. He had to protect them…

The man approached Arissa, and she screamed and swung the fishbowl at the man. It was too awkwardly sized for her to aim well and it only glanced across his temple. He shook his head and then slapped her across the face.

Arissa! Nathan crawled toward them, his leg useless and trembling.

She had fallen to her knees with the blow, and he heard the clatter of her cell phone dropping to the floor. Charity, standing beside her, screamed in a terrified, high-pitched wail, her tiny arms reaching around her aunt.

And then the man grabbed *Charity*.

The little girl kicked and twisted in his arms, causing him to hesitate and try to get a better grip. Then the second man appeared from a different direction, saying something in Filipino. He glanced at Nathan with a look of contempt, then turned away, ignoring him.

Nathan continued toward them, grabbing at a broomstick on the floor.

The first man finally locked his arm firmly around Charity's waist, keeping his body clear of her kicking feet and withstanding her flailing arms. The second man grabbed

Arissa by the arm and tried to drag her toward the door.

She lashed out with a fist that missed his nose by barely an inch. His grip on her arm tightened as he shook her. He said something harsh in Filipino. Arissa responded by drawing back and jabbing again with her fist. This time her blow connected with his chin and he jerked back, more surprised than hurt.

Nathan swept the broom forward, swinging in a wide arc at both of the men's feet. The unexpected blow made the first man stagger and drop Charity.

Nathan didn't pause but swung again, this time hitting the second man harder. That man's grip on Arissa's arm must have loosened because she ripped herself away and dove for Charity, shielding her with her body.

Nathan rose to a sitting position. The first man approached him, his lip curled in a sneer at Nathan's vulnerability.

Nathan jabbed hard with the end of the broom right at the man's throat.

He stumbled back in agony, clutching his neck, a gurgling sound coming from his open mouth.

Arissa was on her feet, reaching inside a nearby box. In a flash she'd hit the other man with the heavy metal stapler in her hand. He grunted in surprise, but it was all the distraction Nathan needed to again sweep the broom under his feet, knocking him to the ground. Nathan lunged forward and jabbed hard at his jaw, and the man passed out from the blow.

The other one was still doubled over, clawing at his throat. Nathan rose up on one knee and threw a roundhouse punch that made him slump to the ground.

Arissa reached for Charity. "Are you all right, *nene?*" Her eyes fell on her cell phone on the floor. She paused, then reached for it.

"Leave it!" Nathan hissed to her.

She ignored him, grabbing the phone and dialing. But strangely, she didn't say anything. Whoever she called spoke a few short sentences to her, the tinny voice barely audible to Nathan.

Then a third man's voice called from the front of the storage unit, and Nathan heard his footsteps approaching, no effort made to be quiet.

Arissa knelt beside Nathan and whispered, "Can you stand?"

He nodded, getting to his feet. Pain stabbed through his leg but he gritted his teeth and hobbled a few footsteps.

Arissa grabbed Charity, ignoring her cries, and hurried to the back of the storage unit. She lay the phone on the ground, then fumbled with the lever on the large metal rolling door.

"They're probably outside," Nathan said. "They'll be onto us in a second." He couldn't run with his leg, but maybe he could cover them with gunfire. But he was almost certain the gang members kept at least someone covering his car.

"I know." Arissa grunted as she unlocked the door lever. She picked up the phone and said to the caller, "Ready."

Nathan heard her caller shout, "Go!"

Arissa swiftly pocketed the phone, then

hauled the rolling door upward. It rattled open with a sound that filled the small storage unit.

At the same time, Nathan heard the roar of a huge engine, the squeal of tires. On the other side of the open door, a shadow fell across the light of a flood lamp.

Arissa darted out, her hand firmly holding Charity. Nathan brought up the rear, the pain screaming behind his clenched teeth as he limped behind them.

A massive SUV was right in front of the storage unit door and Tito had opened the passenger door, his eyes wide. "Get in!" he shouted as bullets began flying. He ducked, and Nathan heard the sound of shots hitting the car frame.

Arissa shoved Charity into the front, which had a bench seat, and scrambled in after her. Nathan yanked open the back door and dove inside. "Go!" he yelled to Tito.

Tito hit the accelerator and they jerked forward, the open back door flapping as the SUV made a sharp turn to head out of the parking lot. More bullets hit the car and one spidered the back window. Arissa and Charity both screamed.

Nathan dug his fingers into the foam seats as his body flopped sideways with the motion of the SUV. There was a huge bump that sent him weightless for a split second before he dropped and rolled to the floor.

Then the SUV straightened and roared off, and the sound of bullets stopped.

Nathan sat up and reached to close the open door. "Everyone okay—?" The sudden pain in his arm felt like a red-hot poker sticking into his bicep. He bit back a groan, but Arissa heard him and looked back.

"What's wrong?" Then her eyes widened and she began scrambling into the rear of the SUV.

"What are you—" he mumbled.

"Nathan, you were hit."

He looked stupidly down at his left arm, coated with blood. Arissa grabbed a T-shirt on the floor behind Tito's seat and applied pressure. The pain exploded from his arm, and coupled with the sharp throbbing from his injured leg, he felt like his body was being ripped apart.

"We need to get to a hospital," Arissa said.

"No." Nathan groaned out the word. "The hospital would report a bullet wound, and we don't know who might be an LAPD mole for the LSLs."

"Nathan, you're going to bleed to death." Arissa's low voice shook.

"Does Tito know anyone…?" he murmured.

Arissa spoke to her cousin. "Tito, do you know anyone who could patch up a bullet wound, no questions asked?"

He turned to briefly give her a look that was both panicked and annoyed. "I don't run with people who get shot."

"A nurse? A doctor?"

He thought a few moments, then shook his head. "Sorry, Arissa. I have a couple doctor friends, but they're up in northern California."

Northern California… "Monica," Nathan rasped. "Shaun's girlfriend is a nurse."

"Shaun O'Neill? Liam's brother? But he's

up in Sonoma." Arissa frowned at him. "That's *seven hours* away."

"I'll call him. They can meet us halfway in central California somewhere." Both Shaun and Monica would do this for him, he knew.

"You want me to drive to central California?" Tito protested.

"You're not exactly safe in Los Angeles," Arissa snapped at him. "I'm sure they got your license plate number." Then she and her cousin both sobered. "I'm sorry about this, Tito."

"Yeah, thanks," Nathan said to him. "You saved our lives."

"How did they find us? I don't understand." Arissa increased pressure on Nathan's wound.

"I think I know," Tito said. "When I got to the storage facility, I saw the gang members' cars, but I recognized the Honda Accord."

"We saw that car when we entered the building," Arissa said. "He was blasting his stereo."

"I thought I heard him come back while

we were inside, but I couldn't be sure," Nathan said.

"He's Mikey, the younger brother of this girl I dated a few months ago," Tito said. "He wanted to get into the LSLs."

"He was probably scoping out the storage facility to see if we'd show up," Nathan said. "He left when he saw us and got the rest of the gang."

"But how did he know my family shares the storage unit?" Arissa asked. "We don't exactly keep it a secret, but it's not something most people know."

"Mikey's sister knew," Tito said grimly.

"Your ex-girlfriend?"

"Sheila Laktaw."

Arissa drew in a breath. "I know her. My parents know her, too."

"Arissa, your mom asked me to get something and give it to my mom. Sheila was with me at the time so I dragged her along and she found out your parents share Mom's storage unit. If the gang made it known they were looking for you, Sheila probably went to her brother with the info about the storage unit so he could get in favor with the gang leaders."

"That would explain why Mikey was staking out the storage facility." Arissa shook her head. "I should have realized that if one of *my* exes knew about the storage unit, there was a chance one of my cousins' friends would know about it, too."

"It's not your job to be paranoid," Nathan said. "It's mine." And he'd failed them.

Tito stopped off and got some first-aid supplies, including a cleaner length of cloth for Arissa to apply pressure to Nathan's wound. The bleeding slowed considerably. He called Shaun and arranged to meet him and Monica in a few hours.

Tito headed north. None of them said much on the drive, which suited Nathan fine. His arm and his leg felt like they were being stabbed with every jolt of the car. He tried to massage his leg but it only hurt more. His hands curled into claws as they gripped his thigh above the old injury.

Because of his leg, he had almost lost both Arissa and Charity. Because of his leg, the attacker had been able to cripple him ridiculously easily. He'd had to crawl toward them, underestimated by the two men. He'd had to fight from the floor, and he'd had to rely on Arissa's help to protect them all.

Next time, he'd be even less help. Arissa had come to him for protection and he'd only barely been able to save their lives. His fingertips dug into his leg, but he welcomed the pain this time because it fueled his anger. He had once been whole and competent and dangerous to his enemies. Now he was a joke. That day in the chop shop, he hadn't just been hit by a bullet. His life had been shattered.

And not by the gang member who had shot him. By God, who had completely abandoned him.

So he had abandoned God.

Didn't this simply underscore the fact that God didn't care about him?

God sent Tito.

Somehow, the thought made him even more angry. God had sent Tito, but He couldn't have shifted that bullet in the chop shop just a few inches so it would damage repairable flesh rather than irreparably splintering his femur? Did God just have it in for him?

His anger, coupled with his guilt that he couldn't better protect Arissa and Charity, felt like a black cesspool sucking him under. He should never have assumed the storage unit was safe just because they'd visited once without incident. He should have been more wary, should have questioned if one of Arissa's relatives had somehow let it slip about the unit. Even if the gang didn't know which one, if they suspected Arissa had something of Mark's, they could assume Arissa might visit the storage facility.

But in the storage unit, when he'd been almost blinded by pain, he had nevertheless seen the gang member grab *Charity* first, not Arissa. The two men had been intending to take them *both*.

Which meant that all their earlier assumptions might be false. They had assumed that the gang thought Arissa knew something about Mark, or had some item of his that they needed.

But the gang needed *Charity*. It could be they planned to use her to get Arissa to co-operate, but it could also mean something he hadn't thought of before.

It could mean the gang needed something that Mark had passed down to his daughter.

NINE

"We're here." Tito took the off-ramp from the freeway to the rest stop where they had agreed to meet Shaun and Monica.

Arissa turned in her seat to ask Nathan, "What car do they drive?"

He shifted and winced. "I don't remember Monica's car, but Shaun drives an extended-cab pickup."

Arissa scanned the parking lot, and at this time of night it was almost empty except for an SUV and two minivans. "I guess they're not here yet."

"I'll text him." Nathan got out his cell phone. Before, he hadn't used his left arm at all, but now he seemed able to move his forearm and use his hand almost the same as normal.

Tito parked and unbuckled his seat belt.

"I'm going to use the bathroom." He exited the car and headed to the dimly lit building.

Nathan looked up from his phone. "Shaun says he's about fifteen minutes away, according to his GPS unit."

"Let me look at your arm again." Since Charity was now asleep in the backseat, Arissa couldn't climb over as she had before, so she got out of the car. A stiff wind cut through her light jacket and made her hurry around to his side of the vehicle to open his door, which shielded her from the wind.

In the light from the nearby streetlamp, his face looked pale. She touched his forehead, which was cool although not yet clammy. Not that she'd know what to do if it had been clammy. The wound seemed to have stopped bleeding. It was a deep gash, long and angry red. Arissa had been profoundly grateful it hadn't been a hole in his arm like she'd feared when she'd first seen the blood. She gently replaced the bandage. "Monica will be here soon and she'll take care of you. How's your leg?"

He turned his head away from her, and he started to shrug but stopped the motion with a sharp intake of breath. Tonight, his leg had been wounded for her, and he had been shot for her.

He had been *shot* for her.

She knew that he'd have been willing to die for them. He had kept attacking those men, even though his leg hadn't been able to hold him, even though all he had was his wits, his strength and a broom.

How could she ever have thought he'd fail her like her previous boyfriends? He hadn't walked away at any time during the past few days, even when the danger had mounted. He had never wavered in being their protector.

It had taken so much of him physically, and she felt stupid for not realizing how the loss of his leg strength would pain him both physically and emotionally. Every time he'd stumbled, he'd reacted like a wounded dog. For a man who was so strong, so brave, so dedicated to protecting others, every time his leg had failed him must have been as painful as a blow.

She suddenly recalled the day in his hospital room, when he'd said such angry, bitter things to her—calling Mark a mole, blaming her brother for his leg, telling her to get out, he never wanted to see her again. The memory still hurt, but it was only a pinch now, and she thought she might understand why he'd reacted that way. He wouldn't exactly have been in a calm frame of mind after being told he may never walk again, and then to have the sister of the man indirectly responsible show up...

Yes, she could finally understand his reaction, and it gave her a measure of peace she hadn't felt about it before. She touched him again, this time on his cheek. "Thank you, Nathan."

"Don't thank me," he growled and pulled away from her hand.

His answer sparked annoyance. "So it would have been better for me and Charity to be kidnapped? Again?"

That got him to look at her, although it

was with surprise and a similar annoyance. "That's not what I meant and you know it."

"Why are you acting as if what you did for us was so terrible?" she shot back. "There were two of them and I couldn't have fought them both off by myself."

The annoyance faded from his eyes, but he dropped his gaze.

She stood there in silence a long while, shivering in the wisps of wind that found her around the shield of the open door. She was about to step back and close the door when she suddenly burst out, "Nathan, are you ever going to forgive me? Forgive my family?"

She hadn't intended to say anything like that, but now that it was out, she searched his face, searched his eyes for her answer. His mouth could say anything, but she knew his eyes wouldn't lie to her.

Right now, his eyes were startled. Then they slid away. "What do you mean?"

"Are you ever going to forgive me for coming to you when the gang was after us? For putting your family in danger, for getting you injured again?"

"I'm not mad at you for that—"

"Are you ever going to forgive me and my family for not knowing Mark was a mole?"

He stared at her, his mouth cracked open. "I don't blame you."

"Are you sure about that?"

He sighed. "I don't mean to make you feel like I blame you for what your brother did. It'll just take a while for me to forgive Mark."

She stared at her shoes. "I understand."

She suddenly felt his hand against her cheek and looked up to see his eyes glittering dark gray in the feeble parking lot lights.

"Arissa." It was as if he said a hundred words with her name, words of pleading, frustration, sorrow, longing. His eyes dropped to her lips, and her breath caught in her throat. He leaned forward…

Then jerked backward, pushing her away. His face clouded. "I don't want your pity."

She was so angry, she was ready to bop him in the nose the way she'd swung at the man in the storage unit, but a flash of head-lights and the soft purr of an engine pre-vented her. She looked up at an extended-cab pickup truck that headed toward them, park-ing next to Tito's SUV.

Tito came up to them as a tall man exited the truck, and a dark-haired woman stepped from exited the passenger-side door while holding a lumpy satchel.

"Thanks for coming. I'm Arissa, and this is my cousin, Tito."

"I'm Shaun and this is Monica," the man said, but immediately turned to Nathan and said in a low voice, "How're you doing, old man?"

"Stop talking to me like I'm dying," Na-than snapped.

Shaun grinned.

"Let me move Charity to the front seat so you can climb into the truck to examine him." Arissa went to the other side and ex-tricated a sleepily protesting Charity, set-tling her in the front seat, where she curled up into a ball and went back to sleep.

"Thanks." Monica climbed into the SUV

to examine Nathan's arm. "I wish you'd let us meet at some nice, brightly lit McDonald's," she grumbled.

"Cameras," Shaun and Nathan said at the same time.

"You law-enforcement guys are so paranoid." Monica got a good look at the wound. "Just a graze."

Just a graze? It had seemed like an awful lot of blood.

"Don't get me wrong, you won't be swimming the butterfly stroke anytime soon," Monica said. "But at least the wound is minor enough that it wasn't the height of stupidity for you to drive *three-and-a-half hours* for someone to dress it."

Arissa tried to hide her smile but failed. Nathan glared at her, which only made her smile more. "I think I like your friends, Nathan."

Monica smiled at her. "I think I like you, too."

Nathan rolled his eyes.

"So you want to tell me why the LSLs shot at you?" Shaun asked.

"I'm surprised they shot at all," Arissa

said. "It's apparent they need both me and Charity alive."

"For what?" Shaun asked.

Nathan nodded at her. "I didn't expect them to grab Charity first, but it was obvious they needed her even more than they needed you."

"Which means the reason they're after us might have to do with something Charity might have inherited from her father," Arissa said. "The problem is that she didn't *get* anything from Mark. He didn't have her in his will."

"Anyone else he mentioned in the will?" Nathan asked. "Something he gave to someone else?"

She shook her head. "He gave everything to our parents. He didn't even mention me in the will."

Nathan dropped his head back against the headrest, then winced as Monica did something to his arm.

"When the gang members first captured us—"

"The LSL gang captured you?" Shaun demanded.

"They took us off the street near my parents' grocery store in broad daylight. I woke up in a dingy house. I heard the two men say something like, they had taken both of us because they hadn't wanted to leave 'her' screaming in the street. I thought at the time they meant Charity, but I'm guessing now that they meant me."

"They may not have thought they needed to take you before," Nathan said, "but they definitely needed you tonight. Otherwise they could have left you in the storage unit when they grabbed Charity."

"So maybe it's not something Charity inherited," Shaun said.

Nathan nodded. "Maybe it's something she's entitled to as Mark's daughter, but they need you because you're her legal guardian."

Arissa met Nathan's eyes. "The safe deposit box?"

Shaun, however, looked skeptical. "Arissa, you or your parents could have eventually gotten access to Mark's safe deposit box since he left your parents everything he owned."

"He's right," Nathan said. "Besides, I don't think the gang knows about the safe deposit box."

She had forgotten about that. "Yes, the teller wasn't suspicious like she probably would have been if someone else had already tried to get into the box and failed."

"And, if they knew about the bank, the best way to capture you again would have been to camp outside that bank and wait for you," Shaun said.

With his last words sounded a beep, and Nathan stared in surprise at his cell phone. "I got a text from Steve."

The name rang a bell for Arissa. "Steve, the detective in the LAPD? But I thought you suspected him of being a mole?"

"Another one?" Shaun said.

"He hasn't done anything to make it obvious he's a mole," Nathan said quickly. "It was just an uncomfortable feeling I had. And I didn't want to be careless and trust him completely when I suspect someone in the LAPD is helping the LSLs."

"What does Steve want?"

"If I'm awake, he has info on the LSLs."

Shaun frowned. "He's texting you at this time of night, a few hours after the LSLs attacked you?"

Arissa bit her lip. The timing was certainly coincidental. "He doesn't know you're with me, does he?"

"No, I didn't tell him anything about you."

"Maybe you should call him." Arissa licked her chapped lip. "He might have some useful information."

"Or he might try to pump you about where you are," Shaun said.

Monica said, "There, I'm done with your shoulder. How's your leg?"

"It's fine," he grunted, and shifted his leg slightly away from her.

Monica didn't respond right away, simply gave him a kind look that wasn't concerned enough to embarrass him. Finally she said in a low voice, "I can give you something for the pain, if you want."

He pressed his lips together for a few terse seconds, then jerked his head in a nod.

"Are you going to call Steve?" Shaun asked.

Nathan pondered that for a while, then said, "Yes." He dialed, putting the phone on speakerphone.

"Hey, Nathan." The man's voice had a lilt, as if he was normally fun-loving and easygoing, but now he had a serious tension to his words. "I'm glad you're up. I just heard something from a detective who came back from some undercover work tonight."

"Was he undercover with the LSLs?"

"No, nothing like that. But he heard some rumors being spread around by a rival gang. When we talked earlier, you asked if there had been any rumblings about the LSLs uprooting and heading north. At the time I thought it was far-fetched, but I was working late tonight and Detective Kim came in. He said that there *are* rumors that the LSLs are moving north."

North? Sonoma? Was this why Mark was in Sonoma?

"Does he know where?" Nathan asked.

"No, and a lot of people discredit the rumors because it's such a huge move for a drug gang. But after what you said, I thought you ought to know."

"I appreciate that, Steve."

"I hope you don't mind, I've been keeping my ear open about anything else to do with the LSLs. Mostly just the normal stuff, but something came up earlier today. I wasn't sure if it means anything, but after hearing this about the LSLs..." Steve coughed. "Well, I guess I'll just tell you. Your ex-partner, Mark Tiong? He was killed by LSLs, right?"

Arissa began to feel a tightness in her chest. She pressed her lips together.

"Yeah," Nathan said.

"His sister is wanted for questioning."

What? Arissa clapped a hand to her mouth. Her fingers dug into her cheeks.

"For what?" Nathan asked harshly.

"A young woman, Malaya, is missing. They were friends, apparently."

Her parents had told her about Malaya. But why did they want to talk to Arissa? Just because the two of them were friends?

"The detective thinks Arissa knows where Malaya is?" Nathan asked.

"Maybe. The girl's parents called—they're out of town, but they rattled some cages even though she's been gone only a couple days. There isn't much to go on, but the officer sent to Malaya's house just found Arissa's cell phone in there, and the last call to the phone was from an LSL gang member."

Arissa drew in a sharp breath. How could that be? She'd completely destroyed her cell phone before heading north—took out the battery, smashed the SIM card, and threw the pieces out the window of her car when she was on the freeway.

But…her *old* cell phone, the one she had before which didn't have internet accessibility like her new Smartphone, had still worked. The old SIM card hadn't been compatible with her new phone, so she'd left it in and had been able to sync her new Smartphone with her computer to transfer over her contacts. And it had been in her parents' apartment—she'd left it in the bedroom in case her mom's ancient cell phone suddenly up and died. She hadn't thought to destroy it. Instead, she'd left it to be used by the LSLs to frame her.

Nathan's answer was in a cool voice. "I didn't think Arissa was close to any of the gang, on account of her brother."

"Yeah, me too, but they have to investigate. There aren't any other leads." Steve paused, then said, "You knew her pretty well, didn't you?"

Nathan hesitated a fraction of a second before answering, "Yeah, I knew her."

"If you know where she might be, you should tell her to come in."

Arissa bit her lip and tasted blood.

Steve continued, "If she's innocent, then it shouldn't be a problem."

Nathan's eyes narrowed as he regarded the cell phone. "Steve, I've got to go. My mom's complaining I'm on the phone so late."

"Oh, sorry." Steve's voice became jovial. "Say hi to your mom for me. You're in… Mendocino, right?"

"Sacramento," Nathan said smoothly, but Arissa heard the edge to his voice.

"Oh, that's right, that's what you said."

"Bye, Steve. Thanks for the info."

"Boy, I didn't expect you to be right about the LSLs. Bye, Nathan."

As soon as he disconnected the call, Arissa's knees buckled, and she grabbed the frame of the car to keep herself standing. Being framed by the LSLs suddenly seemed so much worse. She had nowhere to go.

How could she possibly protect Charity against the LSLs? Even with Nathan's help, they barely stayed one step ahead of the gang. She felt stretched thin, like a rubber band about to break.

"Aunt Rissa, why'd Uncle Tito have to go?"

Nathan glanced around First Sonoma Bank at all the customers who overheard Charity's question to her aunt and then shot Arissa a warning glance, but he shouldn't have worried.

"Uncle Tito had to go home, *nene*." Arissa tried to smile, but it was strained.

Nathan knew she was worried about Tito, but he had deliberately chosen that rest stop because it was near the junctions of several highways. After Shaun helped Tito disable the GPS chip on his SUV, Arissa's cousin had kissed her and Charity goodbye and then headed back south, intending to shoot east across the northern portion of Los Angeles and head toward Phoenix, where he had a few friends.

"But I wanted him to stay with us." Charity pouted. "I want Grandma and Grandpa, too."

Her rising voice made Nathan glance around them again. They'd been extra careful in coming to the bank this morning, watching for any gang members who might be waiting for them, but Nathan hadn't seen anyone suspicious. However, he also didn't want to draw more attention to themselves, and Charity's plaintive voice struck a chord in him that he didn't understand or want to investigate too closely.

He knelt in front of her and caressed her cheek with his hand. "*Nene,* don't you like being with Uncle Nathan? You're going to make me think you don't want me around."

She flung her tiny arms around his neck and squeezed. "I want you here, Uncle Nathan. Don't leave."

The sob at the end of her word made him hug her back a little tighter. "I won't."

In holding the small body, he marveled at how well she was holding up considering all the terrible things she'd had to endure. But he also felt a pang of guilt that he might have to leave them if they had to skip town and go into hiding. How would it affect her to have him break his word to her?

It would feel like Nathan felt when he'd seen Mark pass that folder to the LSL gang member.

He closed his eyes tightly for a moment before releasing Charity. He hoped they wouldn't need to disappear. He'd do everything he could to keep it from coming to that. But what if it did? His mind shied away from the possibilities, the ways his life could change, the way those changes would hurt more and more the deeper he'd let these two people into his heart.

He cleared his throat and rose to his feet.

"Try not to attract attention," he said gruffly to Arissa.

Her brown eyes blinked with hurt, then it was gone and she turned away from him.

He was exhausted. After arriving back at Liam's in the early morning hours, he'd taken the two boxes of Mark's things to Mr. Brummel's side of the duplex and pored over the paperwork again for an hour, trying to see if there was something he'd missed. He'd finally fallen asleep with the paper under his cheek, and Liam had shaken him awake midmorning.

A teller freed up and they approached. Arissa provided the same documents she'd given the first time and asked to see the safe deposit box. This teller scrutinized the documents less than the first one had. After a moment she indicated they should follow her and she led them behind the front desk to the back.

The safe deposit vault was tiny and almost claustrophobic. Arissa produced the key and the teller produced the bank's master key, and with two quick twists the door was unlocked and the box slid out. Arissa held it close to her while Nathan held Charity's hand as the teller showed them to a small windowless room next to the vault. "Just come out and let me know when you want to put the box back," the teller said before closing the door and leaving them alone.

They sat at the rickety table in the center of the room. As Arissa set down the box, something softly thumped inside.

Nathan's heart rate climbed. This had to be related to what the gang wanted with Charity. He couldn't think of any other reason Mark would bother to take out a safe deposit box when he obviously had had an unknown apartment somewhere in Sonoma to hide his secrets in. This had to be something extraordinarily special, something that would enable Nathan to bring in the police and free Arissa and Charity from the LSLs forever.

She flipped open the top of the metal box with hands that shook. Charity, sitting next to her, leaned over eagerly to peek over the edge and see what was inside.

Arissa's brow creased. Nathan's stomach flipped.

She pulled out a small velvet jeweler's box.

In a flash, Nathan realized he'd been entirely wrong.

Arissa didn't know whether to cry or laugh.

She opened the jeweler's box and the diamond engagement ring sparkled up at her, brilliant even in the feeble fluorescent lights of the room.

"He was going to propose." Her voice was soft.

"Pretty," Charity said. "Can I see?"

Arissa hesitated, then plucked out the ring and gave it to her. It belonged to her now, the last—the only—gift from her father.

Charity handled the ring carefully despite her fumbling fingers. The diamond fascinated her, maybe because she'd probably never seen one. Mom had sold her rings long ago, and Arissa had also sold any jewelry she had had of any value. Charity might have seen diamonds when she lived with her mother's parents, but Arissa wasn't certain she would remember if she had. Charity's wide brown eyes crossed as she held up the ring in front of her nose. Her mouth hung open as she saw the diamond catch the light in a prism of color.

"Charity, could I see it?" Nathan held out his hand. His voice had an edge of anxiety. Charity slowly handed it to him, and he looked it over, squinting inside the band.

"Is there an inscription?" Arissa asked.

"'Mark and Jemma forever.'"

"He probably intended to propose soon because her official due date had been a month after he died." Arissa remembered Johnny Capuno's bitter words as he told her about his sister's death three years earlier, giving birth to a cop's child. "Johnny…" She glanced at Charity, not wanting her to know how much her uncle hadn't wanted her. "Johnny said that the events at the chop shop made her go into labor early."

"He told you this when he brought you Charity?"

She nodded.

"He obviously didn't know at the time that the gang needed Charity for something." Nathan almost smiled. "The LSL leaders probably weren't too happy with him for giving her to you."

Johnny had told Arissa that if she didn't take Charity, he'd dump her at the nearest orphanage. What kind of a person would do that to a three-year-old?

Nathan looked at the ring. "Johnny wouldn't have been happy about Mark proposing to his sister."

The implications suddenly hit her like a dash of cold water. "Oh my goodness. What kind of implications would there have been?"

"The LAPD wouldn't have been happy about him marrying the sister of the captain of a dangerous gang. I don't know exactly what they might do in a situation like that."

"Even though he was giving information to the gang, the LSLs wouldn't have been happy about it, either." Arissa patted Charity's shoulder as Nathan gave the ring back to the little girl. "If it cost Mark his job at the LAPD, they'd have no use for him."

"Is there anything else in the box?"

"Just this." She took out the jeweler's receipt for the ring and an authenticity certificate for the diamond. "I had hoped for so much more."

Nathan flipped through the paper. "If the LSLs don't need Charity to get access to this safe deposit box, what do they need her for?"

"Maybe they didn't know what was in the box and needed to check?"

"I don't think they'd go through so much trouble to try to kidnap her when they didn't know what was actually in the box."

"Unless what they're looking for is extremely important to them, and they knew Mark hid it somewhere. They'd look everywhere possible for it."

"It must not have been something they missed right away, because Johnny..." Nathan cut himself off and glanced at Charity. "And they waited three years after Mark's death."

"So what would be so important now but not important enough to miss three years ago?"

Nathan shook his head. "Money they would miss right away. Same thing with drugs."

"All he gave them was information. What did he have that they need so badly now?"

The two of them were silent until Charity dropped the ring on the floor and it clinked with a delicate tinkle. Arissa picked it up and returned it to the jeweler's box, then set it in the safe deposit box. "This is just a dead end."

"Mark might have another bank account somewhere."

"How likely is that?" Arissa closed the lid on the safe deposit box, feeling as empty as the clang of the metal on metal. "I'm guessing whatever the gang is so desperate to get was in Mark's apartment. And it's long gone by now, tossed out by some unsuspecting landlord."

"No, because the gang needs…her…for some reason—" Nathan glanced at Charity but she didn't seem to be listening "—and they don't need her if they think the information is in a nonsecure location like an apartment."

"But where? And what?"

"That's the million-dollar question."

They called the teller, who locked the safe deposit box back in the vault and escorted them out to the main area of the bank.

They drove back to Liam's in silence, although Arissa felt as if she were filled with ice water, making her shiver. What could they do next? What was left but to run away—and keep running?

Nathan turned into the driveway that would lead to the duplexes but then jerked the car to a halt. The seat belt sliced across her chest. She coughed. "What's wrong?"

Nathan pointed ahead of them. Parked in the middle of the driveway, farther down, was a familiar black BMW SUV.

"They're..." She gulped. "They're parked in front of Liam's duplex."

"Hang on. I don't think they've seen us." Nathan twisted around and backed out of the driveway, getting onto the main road and retracing the way they'd come.

"Where are you going? We can't leave Liam there."

"We're not."

He only drove a few hundred yards before pulling to the side of the road in front of a closed gate into a vineyard, used for farm vehicles. Nathan parked so that he didn't block the gate, then got out. "Stay here."

She wasn't entirely comfortable with that. Nathan was the only one carrying a weapon— if the gang members spotted his car and recognized it, she and Charity would be sitting ducks. But she also wasn't stupid enough to want to walk into a duplex where gang members might be waiting for them. "Leave me the car keys."

He paused, then nodded. "You're right, you might need them." He tossed them to her, then took off limping down the road toward Liam's house.

Charity had started whimpering at Nathan's abrupt driving, but now she began crying in earnest so Arissa got out and opened the back door. "It's all right, *nene*."

She soothed her niece and even managed to distract her with some hand games.

And then she saw the extended-cab pickup truck, and the familiar driver as it passed her on the road, heading toward Liam's house. *Shaun.*

Oh, no. She grabbed at her cell phone, then realized she didn't know Shaun's cell number. She cried out in frustration as she realized she didn't have Nathan's number either since she hadn't had a reason to call him.

Should she go after them? No, that would be completely foolish. But could she sit here and do nothing, knowing Nathan and Liam and the people in his house didn't know Shaun was about to burst in on them?

Had Nathan called the police? There, something she could do. She dialed 9–1–1 and asked the dispatcher to put her through to Detective Carter, that it was an emergency involving Nathan Fischer and Shaun O'Neill. The female dispatcher was prompt and put her through without questioning her. If the woman was from Sonoma, she probably knew the Fischers and O'Neills.

"Yes?" Detective Carter's gravelly voice was urgent.

"It's Arissa Tiong. Nathan and I have been staying with Liam O'Neill and we discovered the gang member's SUV outside his house. Nathan parked down the road and ran to help Liam, but I just saw Shaun O'Neill driving toward Liam's house. He doesn't know the gang members are there." Her voice was rising with her panic, and she struggled to keep control of herself.

"Are you in a safe place?" Detective Carter asked.

"Yes."

"Where's Liam's house?"

She gave him the address and also told him where Nathan's car was located.

Detective Carter said something to someone else, then told her, "Nathan already called it in so officers will be there soon. Don't move. I'll send a car to your location, too."

Arissa left Charity fussing in the car and walked a little ways down the road, staring at the line of duplexes. She couldn't see much through the rows of grapevines. Was Nathan all right? Was Liam at home? How long before the police officers got there?

Then suddenly the *crack!* of a gunshot split the air.

TEN

Nathan snuck up on Liam's duplex by hiding behind the hedge, his gun at the ready. He peered through a triangular gap in the branches, but didn't see anything.

However, he heard plenty. The sound of crashing and smashing came from Liam's side of the duplex. The gang members were searching the place, or perhaps just destroying everything to make a point, to instill fear.

Liam wasn't easily scared, and neither was Nathan.

Was Liam inside? He shifted position to see around the BMW SUV, but Liam's carport was empty. He exhaled a shaky breath.

He'd called the police already and they should be here soon. Maybe he could find out how many gang members there were inside the house—more than one, it sounded like, but just two? Or three?

Nathan slipped through the triangular break in the hedge and ran, keeping low to the ground, around Mr. Brummel's side of the duplex and toward the rear. His leg protested. He ignored it. Liam's back door had a screen door, but it sagged open on broken hinges. The door itself had a doggie door covered by a rubber flap near the bottom. Nathan kept close to the walls as he crept nearer. He got on his stomach and slowly, quietly lifted the rubber doggie door flap to look inside.

Because Liam's kitchen was open to the living room, Nathan had a clear view of the man looking at Liam's laptop—the same man from the rest stop, the same man they'd seen in the parking lot outside the hardware store. They hadn't left Sonoma.

It sounded like someone else was trashing the one bedroom. The first man said something in Filipino to the person in the bedroom, and the second man exited the room as he responded. There didn't seem to be anyone else in the house.

Then Nathan heard the deep growl of a car engine coming up the driveway. No, not a car—a truck or an SUV.

His first thought was that it was Liam returning, and his pulse beat hard against his throat. But no, Liam's truck was old and the engine coughed and sputtered. This engine purred and growled. In fact, it sounded like Shaun's truck…

Oh, no.

Nathan got to his feet, although his leg ached from the running and his shoulder burned. He crept back along the side of the house to peek around the corner toward the front.

Shaun had just exited his truck and was approaching Liam's house.

Nathan waved his arm to get his attention, mouthing for him to get back, making his movements frantic and urgent.

Shaun saw, tensed, then bolted back to the truck.

At that moment, one of the gang members burst out of the front door and fired at Shaun.

Nathan fired back but missed. The recoil slammed through his injured shoulder, and he inhaled sharply.

He looked up and saw Shaun on the ground. Not moving.

The gang member had ducked back inside the house, but now a hand holding a gun snaked out the door. Since Nathan was around the corner, he had a perfect shot and aimed for the man's knuckles.

The man yelled and dropped his gun, disappearing again in the house. There was a space of two heartbeats and then both men ran out of the house, the uninjured one firing in Nathan's direction. Nathan hung behind the corner, but none of the bullets came even close.

The BMW's engine came to life. Nathan looked out to see the two men had jumped into the SUV. It backed down the driveway in a cloud of dirt and gravel, barely missing Shaun's form on the ground before it shifted out onto the street and drove away.

Nathan ran to Shaun, heedless of the pain stabbing his thigh with each step. "Shaun!" There was blood blossoming along the side of his torso. Had the bullet gone clean through his abdomen? Had it hit a vital organ? Nathan yanked off his shirt and pressed it to the wound.

Please, not Shaun. Not the man who'd become such a good friend since he'd moved back to Sonoma. Not the one person who kept him sane when his injury made him want to hermit himself away. Nathan pulled out his cell phone and told the dispatcher to send an ambulance.

Shaun groaned as Nathan continued to apply pressure. "Did you get them?" he asked in a thready voice.

Nathan had to ungrit his teeth before answering. "No."

"Same guys?"

"Yeah."

Shaun passed out just as Nathan heard sirens in the distance.

It was all his fault.

No. It was all God's fault.

He only had to look at Shaun, lying in the hospital bed. What kind of God allowed something like this to happen?

Nathan had only ever tried to do the right thing, and all that had led to was more suffering, more violence. It would have been easier for him to take if it had only been suffering and violence to himself, but it had affected the people he cared about. His closest friend in Sonoma had been shot. What would happen next?

Monica sat beside Shaun, her face white but her voice determinedly cheerful. "It's great news, you dork."

"How is a hole in my side great news?" Shaun's voice was weak, but his smile at Monica was calm and quirky.

"It's not really a hole. It didn't perforate your abdominal cavity."

"It took a chunk out of my amazing stomach muscles. I was going for a six-pack. Now I guess I'll have to settle for a five-pack."

Monica rolled her eyes.

Shaun's father, Patrick O'Neill, stood at the foot of the bed and only gave a tight smile. The twinkle usually in his eye was missing as he gazed at his injured son.

Nathan turned away and walked out of the hospital room. However, at the door he met two uniformed officers, Charlie Granger and Joseph Fong, who had been among the other officers responding to his 9–1–1 call.

"Hi, Nathan," Charlie said. "Sorry I can't chat. I'm here to talk to Shaun, now that he's all patched up."

"And Detective Carter sent me to ask Liam to come see him," Joseph said.

"Liam's not here yet," Nathan told him.

Strangely, Joseph didn't react to that. "Oh. I guess I can stay here to guard Shaun, wait for Liam. Keep an eye on Arissa and Charity, too."

Charlie nudged him with an elbow. "No, you slacker, get back to work."

Joseph grinned at him.

"Oh, and don't worry about someone watching your parents' house," Charlie said. "Detective Carter put another team on it. Good thing, too, or we'd have missed out on responding to your call today."

The two men nodded to Nathan, and Charlie entered the hospital room while Joseph disappeared down the hallway.

Nathan walked out also, but didn't see Arissa or Charity waiting in the nearby chairs. He asked the nurse at the adjacent desk if she'd seen them, and she pointed around a corner.

Arissa sat with Charity in two padded chairs next to a worn box of toys. She looked up as he approached, her eyes darker than normal.

"Shaun's going to be fine," he said.

"I know. I'm worried about you."

Why was she concerned for him when she should be concerned about Shaun? About her parents, about Tito, about her missing friend Malaya? He was tired of being the object of people's pity. He scowled at her.

She blinked, but didn't look away. She patted the empty seat next to her. "Sit down, Nathan."

He didn't want to. He didn't want to admit to himself that his leg ached and he ought to take the weight off of it. He knew his injury wasn't the reason Shaun was hurt, but he wanted to blame someone. Something. Anything.

He sat next to Arissa but only because he knew it wouldn't do him any favors to aggravate his leg when he didn't need to. Then he saw the book in her lap.

A Gideon Bible. She'd probably snagged it from Shaun's bedside table. She had it open although he didn't look closely enough to find out which book she read. The sight of it renewed his anger and he clenched his jaw and turned away.

She misinterpreted his actions. "It's not your fault, Nathan."

But it was his fault. He should never have involved the O'Neills in this. He should have kept them out of it because he knew the situation was dangerous. "Whose fault is it, then?" he said sharply.

"The shooter's?"

"You know that's not what I'm talking about."

"Why does it have to be someone's fault?"

"How can it not be someone's fault? Someone has to take responsibility. There's already too many people not facing the consequences of their actions." Like himself. That should be him in that hospital bed, not Shaun.

"This isn't the same thing." She kept her voice low so as not to alarm Charity, who was talking to a doll with only one arm, but he couldn't miss the urgency in her tone.

"How do you know it's not?"

Her mouth opened but she couldn't answer him.

"You can't know, can you? I used to think that what goes around comes around, that if I did my best to do the right thing, then my life would be better for it. But no matter how hard I try, I keep making the wrong decisions and people get hurt."

"How is it your fault that strangers hurt the people you care about? You didn't fire at Shaun."

"Those men wouldn't have been at Liam's house if not for me."

"For us. So it's my fault, too?" Her eyes glittered with anger and tears.

"Yes!" he burst out. He shot to his feet and turned away from her.

"Don't turn your back on me." Her voice trembled, low and growling. "You did that three years ago. You're not going to do that again."

"Are we going to rehash that now?"

"We never resolved anything in the first place." The Bible thudded to the floor as she also rose to her feet, as if she didn't want to be at a disadvantage. Or maybe she wanted to distance her anger from Charity, who now cast them fearful glances.

He made an effort to lower his voice and calm the tension in the air between them. "I was hurt at the time."

"I know that. I was hurt, too, and I didn't respond the way I should have."

The two of them stepped out of the way of a passing nurse.

"Nathan, all the bad things that happen to you don't mean you've made bad decisions. Was I wrong in taking in Charity? If I hadn't, we wouldn't be in danger. Yet you can't say that it was wrong for me to care about her."

Maybe it had been wrong for her to care about Charity. Maybe it was wrong for him to care about people, because they seemed to be put in harm's way because of his decisions.

"I think…" She hesitated. "I think God has a purpose for everything that happens—"

"Don't talk to me about God," he snapped.

"Are you blaming God for all this?"

"Would you really be surprised if I did?"

She looked like she wanted to say something, but stopped herself.

"Say it," he said.

"No, it's nothing."

"Just say it."

Her lips pressed together as she studied him. Finally she said, "Why are you blaming God for what other people do?"

She'd said something similar earlier, but somehow pulling God into it now made a hot flash of fire burn in his gut. "How can you look at Shaun and still insist God only wants our good? He's God. He could have shifted that bullet an inch or two so it wouldn't hit him."

"How do you know He didn't shift that bullet already?"

"Why not go all the way? Shaun will be out of commission for weeks. Explain to me why God would want Shaun injured this way when He could have prevented it entirely."

"I don't know. I can't explain it because I'm not God."

She shook her head. Something about her face unnerved him. She was uncowed by his anger, and yet instead of getting mad back at him, she looked at him with…

Pity.

He stormed away from her. Her faith upset him. Angered him. Rebuked him. He didn't need that. He was almost through the doors of the hospital before he realized where he was. Then a voice snapped him out of his black reverie.

"Nathan." Liam strode toward him.

"Shaun will be fine. It's a flesh wound in his lower abdominal."

"Yeah, Dad just called to let me know. How's your arm?"

He needed this, this terse conversation about injuries and not feelings. "Monica looked at it a few minutes ago for me. It looks better already."

"Lucky it wasn't more than a graze."

"Yeah." Enough about him. "Did you go back to your house?"

Liam glanced around at the nurses and patients milling around the waiting room, and motioned subtly with his head for them to walk out of the hospital. They maneuvered deeper into the parking lot to a far corner that had a minuscule grassy triangle bordered by flowers, with a bench in the middle. They sat.

"They looked through my computer," Liam said. "They probably would have destroyed it if they'd had time."

"They saw everything, then?"

"Well, here's the thing. The internet history where Arissa logged in to First Sonoma Bank—it seems like they didn't even look at it. They probably thought it was mine and didn't even connect it with Mark. And for my work, I have a lot of different email addresses, so the one of Mark's that Arissa found got lost among all the others I have."

"Could they log in to any of those?"

"No, the browser is not set to remember user names and passwords. It comes with being a skip tracer—I have to be paranoid or I'm not doing my job."

"Could you tell what they might have been looking for? They tore up the bedroom, too."

Liam shook his head. "They were pretty violent, makes me think they might have been destructive just to send a message."

"So maybe what they want from Charity isn't an object she inherited?"

"Can't say. Don't make any assumptions."

Nathan nodded. He was right. "Did they leave any clue as to how they found your home in the first place?"

Liam shook his head.

Nathan exhaled in frustration. "I thought we were being careful."

"You were. No one except Dad and Shaun knew I was back in Sonoma. Even Brady didn't find out until a few days ago, and he knew not to tell anyone."

"You've never had contact with any LSL gang members, have you?"

Liam snorted in disbelief. "Of course not."

"And Shaun…" Suddenly he remembered. "Last year, Shaun asked me to look into police reports about your sister's death down in Los Angeles."

Liam nodded. "He told me about that."

"I asked my friend Steve Thompson to do that for me."

Liam's brows drew together. "The same guy you asked about the LSLs."

"He happened to call right after the LSLs attacked us at the rest stop. The timing was suspicious, and it crossed my mind that he might be a mole and checking up on me, but I didn't say anything to him about Arissa. But if he is in contact with the LSLs, then he already knows the gang is after Arissa and that she's with me."

"And the LSLs know you're in Sonoma, after you were seen coming back from the bank."

"Steve knows I'm friends with Shaun, and that the O'Neills live in Sonoma. Since I'm not at my parents' house, it wouldn't be a huge stretch for him to look at any Sonoma properties owned or rented by O'Neills, on the chance I'd be hiding with one of them." Which he had been.

"That's assuming Steve is the mole."

"Which I'm not entirely sure about," Nathan admitted.

"What about people in Sonoma who might have talked to the LSL guys? They could have been asking around."

Nathan remembered seeing the two gang members talking to the migrant workers gathered at the hardware store parking lot. "Maybe. They might have gotten lucky and talked to someone who knows me or my family. But that person would also have to know Shaun and I are friends."

"Shaun and I are five years apart so we were never in the same school at the same time, but I don't remember the two of you being friends back then."

"We weren't. I didn't actually meet him

until we were both working down south—
me in the LAPD, him on the border patrol."

"So you can probably rule out school
friends you haven't talked to recently."

"I don't exactly tell everyone I see now
that I'm friends with Shaun O'Neill. And I
don't know if my parents would have told
any of their friends." Nathan kicked at the
grass at his feet. "Is it really possible that
the LSL gang members would have somehow managed to speak to someone purely by
chance who knew these things about me?"

"What about someone in Sonoma working for the LSLs?"

Nathan looked at Liam. "A gang member?"

"Not necessarily. Could be someone sym-
pathetic with them, trading something for
something."

"Would the LSLs really have had time to
find an ally here in Sonoma between the
time Arissa escaped and contacted me?"

"Mark was here in Sonoma. I know you
said that he had the excuse that he was visiting an aunt who lives here, but what if that

wasn't the reason he chose to have a bank account here as opposed to somewhere else?"

Nathan remembered his conversation with Steve. "Steve mentioned there are rumors the LSLs are moving north, although he didn't say where. What if they are moving to Sonoma? That wouldn't explain why Mark was here—after all, he was a mole giving them information from the LAPD, not a captain of the gang in charge of their larger plans. But it would explain if the LSLs do have someone here in Sonoma who's working for them. That could be how they found us."

He and Arissa needed to be doubly careful about where they hid next. He asked Liam, "What are you going to do? Where are you going to go now?"

Liam smiled at him but didn't say anything.

"That's right. Never mind." Liam was a skip tracer. He probably already had a safe house set up.

"Do you have any ideas about where you'll be next? I can help if you want."

"I'm not sure. It needs to be somewhere

unconnected with my family so whoever found out we were staying with you can't find us again."

"It's too bad you don't know where Mark's apartment is."

"It's probably been cleaned out and rented to someone else by now." Nathan dug out the key to look at it. "It might not be an apartment at all."

Liam's brows suddenly drew down. "Can I see that?"

Nathan passed the key to Liam.

"This key is pretty new," Liam said. "No dings or scratches. Here's the key to my dad's house." Liam fumbled with his key chain and separated his house key, which was covered in scratches and had remnants of tape stuck to one side. "My key looks like it's been in a bomb blast. Whereas Mark's doesn't."

"He could have gotten a newer apartment."

"Could he really afford it?"

Nathan thought back to his bank account. "He didn't have much money when he first started working with the LSLs, but he got more later. I don't know when he got this apartment. And it could be that the landlord had just replaced the locks with new ones and that's why his key looks so new."

Nathan's cell phone rang, and he recognized the number as Shaun's. "Hello?"

"I can't believe I keep forgetting to get your number on my cell phone," Arissa groused. "I had to use Shaun's phone."

He felt a twinge that he hadn't thought about it earlier. Arissa had mentioned that she hadn't been able to call his cell phone when she saw Shaun driving to Liam's house. "Here it is—"

"Tell me when you get up here to the hospital room."

"I'll be up in a few—"

"I'd like you to come now, if you can."

"Sure. Why?" He rose to his feet and motioned to Liam to join him. They started walking back across the parking lot toward the entrance to the hospital.

"I think I've found a new hideout for us."

Hideout was right. Arissa squinted through the trees. "I'm not seeing it." She could barely see the dirt track Nathan drove along through the forest. "I thought Sonoma was all vineyards and rolling foothills."

"We're not in Sonoma anymore." Nathan paused as the SUV jounced over a rut. "We passed civilization a county ago."

"Ha, ha." Arissa grabbed at the dashboard as the car bounced again. "If Monica wasn't dating your good friend, I'd suspect her of sending us to get lost in the woods."

"How much farther?"

"The cabin's supposed to be coming up soon."

The words had just left her mouth when they turned and saw the brightness of a clearing through the trees. Another turn and they exited the trees to park in front of a tiny wooden cabin.

Arissa got out and unbuckled Charity from the new child's seat they'd had to buy. The SUV, an older model than Nathan's, had been borrowed from one of Patrick O'Neill's friends.

Arissa turned to survey the cabin, which had been Monica Grant's idea. Made of darkened, weathered wood, it had the distinct air of neglect, as Monica had warned. Her aunt's cousins rarely used the vacation cabin, for the simple reason that it had spotty cell phone coverage and didn't have internet access.

"This isn't too bad." Nathan tried to peer into a grimy window. "And it's not so far from a major road that we can still get to Sonoma within an hour."

The front door lock stuck, and Nathan had to strain to open it. It didn't help that his left arm still hurt him and he couldn't use it as fully as he'd like. The lock finally slid back and they entered the cabin.

Dark wood beams crisscrossed the ceiling and glossy wood paneling made the cabin seem a bit like a cave. The effect was enhanced by the dirty windows—only four of them, and small. Arissa eyed the ratty couch, wondering if she had heard a mouse's squeak from its lumpy depths. Dust coated the oak dining table and the cheap Formica counters in the kitchen, which was open to the living room like Liam's place had been.

"How often do Monica's cousins use this place?"

"Not her cousins. It belongs to Monica's aunt Becca's cousin on her mother's side. But they don't use it very often, she said."

"I guess it doesn't matter. As long as it's a safe place for us."

"It should be. The name on the property is Becca's cousin, who has a completely different last name from Becca's."

"Let's start a fire before it gets too cold."

Soon Nathan had a wood-burning fire going in the stone fireplace in the living room, and after placing the screen in front of it, Arissa had Charity playing with her dolls by the roaring blaze. Nathan helped her clean the worst of the dirt and dust from the living room and kitchen. He tackled the two small bedrooms and bathroom while she set about heating up some canned soup to go along with the bread they'd also bought.

She tensed as they sat down to the meal, but she wasn't about to change her habit of saying grace just because of Nathan's bitterness toward God. "Let's pray, *nene*."

Charity immediately folded her hands and bowed her head, and Arissa did also without looking to see what Nathan did. She said a short grace and when she said "Amen," Nathan surprised her by grunting, "Amen" right after her. Old habits died hard, she supposed.

"Aunt Rissa, why couldn't Uncle Liam come with us?" Charity asked.

"He had a new home to go to." He'd been as secretive as a CIA agent about it, too.

"Why did he go to a new home?"

"His old home got...messy."

"I could have helped him clean up." Charity slurped her soup. "I'm good at helping, right, Uncle Nathan? I helped you with the bedroom."

She'd actually only stood in the doorway and watched as Nathan swept the floor, then took the bedcovers stored in the cedar chest outside to shake them out and air them. But he said, "You were a big help." To Arissa he said, "Good thing Monica remembered to send clean sheets with us. There weren't any in the bedrooms."

"You brought in the towels from the car, right?"

He nodded and tore off a piece of bread.

Such a strangely domestic conversation, a marked contrast to the tense last few days. She could almost pretend they were a family sitting down to dinner.

Then Nathan happened to look up at her and meet her eyes. His gaze slid away immediately.

Not quite a family. No, they would probably never be a family. Not with the way Nathan felt about her brother, her faith. What a complete change from three years ago, when Nathan and Mark had been such good friends, when he'd been a strong Christian. It seemed her entire world had turned upside down.

They cleaned up the supper dishes, paired Nathan's new prepaid phone to the wireless hub, and connected the laptop to the internet. Arissa looked at his phone. "Cell coverage is pretty poor."

"As long as it's not nonexistent, I'm fine. Let me check my email..." He grunted.

"What is it?"

"I got an email from Steve Thompson. He said he tried calling my cell phone, but since we got new ones and dumped the old ones, his call didn't go through. He asked me to call him tonight because he has news about the LSLs."

She frowned. "He has impeccable timing."

Nathan exhaled a long, slow breath. "I'm not sure if I should call him."

"He can find your new phone number if you call him, right?"

"That's not a problem. If I keep the call short and shut the phone off after I use it, he can't use its GPS chip to track us." He paused before adding, "Assuming he's a mole for the LSL gang."

"He seems to always call after something significant happens—after we were attacked at the rest stop, after we'd escaped the gang members at the storage facility and now that we're in a new hiding place."

"But what if it's important information? He did tell us about the LSL gang moving north, which might be a significant reason for Mark to have been in Sonoma."

Arissa bit her lip. "If you want to call him, I can take Charity to the other room. The door doesn't close all the way, but I can keep her quiet."

He absently swept his hand over the keyboard without depressing any of the keys. "Okay, I'll give him a call." He retrieved his cell phone while Arissa talked to Charity about being very quiet for a few minutes as she carried her to the bedroom. Her niece tended to be quiet anyway, but Arissa didn't want any sudden outbursts while Nathan was on the phone, especially because the warped bedroom door didn't close properly.

He put the phone on Speaker and dialed. "Hey, Steve, it's Nathan." Arissa knew he put it on speaker so she could listen in.

"Got a new cell phone?"

"Yeah, I dropped my old one while fishing on the lake."

"Oh, sucks for you, buddy."

"So what's up?"

"You know how I told you about Malaya and Arissa?"

"Did the detective in charge ever find Arissa to ask her about her cell phone?"

"No, not as far as I know. But things are looking worse for her."

Arissa tensed.

"How?" Nathan asked, an edge to his voice.

"Malaya's dead."

Malaya? No! Arissa fought to keep in the cries threatening to burst from her.

"She was found this morning. Looked like she'd been tortured." Steve's voice dropped at the end.

Arissa squeezed her eyes shut. Tortured to give the LSLs information about her car.

Then a tiny voice at her ear, "Aunt—"

She immediately wrapped her arms around Charity to muffle her words. She'd let her tension affect her niece, and she couldn't let Steve know they were with Nathan. She bent her head close to whisper, "Remember, we need to be quiet, *nene*."

The little girl nodded against her shoulder, and Arissa released her.

Steve was continuing, "Body was found in LSL territory, so the detective in charge is looking into the gang—the torture looks like their work, anyway."

Arissa cringed at his heartless words, but she had to remember that he didn't know she was listening. Steve thought he was simply talking to a fellow detective about someone neither of them knew.

"But the detective wants to follow up on Arissa's cell phone that was found in Malaya's apartment, since an LSL member had been the last call she received."

"When was the time of death?" Nathan asked.

"She'd been dead at least twenty-four hours. Medical examiner still hasn't made an official report."

"I can't believe that of Arissa," he told Steve in a neutral voice.

"Have you spoken to her recently?"

Nathan regarded the phone with a narrow gaze as he said, "I reported her brother to

IA, remember? I haven't talked to her family since Mark died."

"No, of course. I forgot."

Nathan cleared his throat. "Thanks for telling me, Steve."

"I figured you'd want to know, it being Mark's sister and all. And because you recently saw those LSL gang members. See any more?"

"Nope, just those two."

"If you do, give me a call to let me know. After hearing those rumors, it might be worth it to call in some favors from NorCal law enforcement."

"Yeah, I can see that. Okay." Nathan's voice was light. Arissa couldn't understand how he could manage to sound so casual for Steve's benefit.

"Well, say hi to your parents for me."

Nathan paused a split second before correcting him, "Just my mom's here with me. Dad's with a church group."

"What a good son you are." Steve chuckled. "See ya."

"Bye." Nathan heard a dial tone as Steve hung up the phone.

Arissa didn't understand why, but only when Nathan disconnected the call did her body begin to tremble violently. She took several deep breaths, trying to calm down. She had to be strong for Charity's sake. They were still in danger. She couldn't let the news about Malaya break her.

"You did very well, *nene,*" she said weakly to her niece. "Good job staying quiet."

They returned to the living room, and Charity immediately began babbling to her doll. Arissa sat next to her, not really listening. Her eyes followed Nathan as he took out the cell phone battery and then dumped the phone and battery in the bucket of wash water from the dishes. He glanced at her, but then looked away awkwardly, obviously not sure what to say to her.

She didn't really want to talk just yet. There was a shivering deep in her gut and an icy coldness that began to spread outward. Where was God in all of this? How could she trust Him to protect them when He hadn't protected Malaya? The LSLs had already tortured and killed her friend. Who would be next? Nathan's parents? Hers?

Who else would have to die for her?

"We shouldn't have refused police protection," she said to Nathan.

"Don't second-guess our decision—"

"It seems dumb now that we didn't want the police knowing about Mark until we'd figured out exactly what he was doing. The police could have protected you and your family, at least. I wouldn't worry about the LSLs—"

"Stop it." He gave her a fierce look.

"Why? You're the only one allowed to feel guilty?"

Charity suddenly grew very quiet and her eyes on Arissa and Nathan were wide. Arissa shouldn't let her emotional turmoil and disagreement with Nathan upset her niece. This wasn't her fault. But Arissa's grief was too sharp, her anger too hot, her loneliness and fear too intense. She tried to calm down, but only felt like a pressure cooker on a hot stove.

Nathan gave her a frustrated shrug. "What do you want me to do about this?"

Hold me. Comfort me. Make all the monsters go away. "I don't know. Stop being so mean."

"Mean?" His brows pulled down and he looked even meaner than before.

"My friend is dead and you're being bitter and angry."

He inhaled sharply. It looked like he was counting to ten. "I'm not angry at you. We're in a bad situation here, in case you haven't noticed."

"Can't you see the world isn't conspiring against you?" *Can't you see that our pain should bring us together and not push us apart?*

"Can't you see that maybe the world *is* conspiring against us?"

"No. No." She shook her head, even though she knew she'd been thinking that only a few minutes earlier. She felt so abandoned by God, but to start blaming Him seemed too awful. Too raw.

"When I got shot, I felt betrayed," he ground out. "Not just by Mark, but by God. And I prayed and went to my pastor for counseling, and then came the day the doctor told me I'd never be able to go back to the force, that my career was done." He was massaging his leg, hard, but he seemed not to notice the pain. "I didn't abandon God— He abandoned me."

"He hasn't abandoned us," she said in a hoarse voice. But she felt so very alone.

Nathan exhaled sharply and turned away from her.

"He hasn't," she whispered, too low for Nathan to hear. It felt like she was trying to convince herself.

Nathan crammed his fingers through his fine brown hair, then paced across the small kitchen, pressing his palm to his forehead. Finally he muttered, "I need some air." And he slammed out the back door.

Charity had already grown still beside Arissa, but the noise of Nathan's exit made her start to shake.

"It's all right." Arissa wrapped her arms around her, squeezing her perhaps a bit too tightly. She'd been such a quiet child, especially when she first came to Arissa, that she wondered if she'd heard arguments like this in her mother's parents' home. Just the hint of tension seemed to frighten her. "I'm sorry. This isn't your fault. Don't be sad."

This little girl had become so very precious to her. How could she keep her safe? They had escaped immediate danger for now, but it was always there, one step behind them, snapping at their heels, and Arissa constantly expected it to suddenly bite.

And it wasn't just Charity she had to protect. What about her parents and all the other people who were affected by this? She'd brought danger down on each of them, too.

She might have felt less helpless if she hadn't lost that sense of God's presence. She had felt it for months after first becoming a Christian, but now there was only emptiness.

Oh, Malaya. What have I done?

"Aunt Rissa, why are you crying?"

She hadn't even realized the flow of her tears. She wiped at her face with her sleeve. "I'm fine." Her heart was breaking. "Tell me a story about this doll." She picked up one with blond hair streaked with pink where some child had colored it with a red marker.

She listened with only half an ear to her niece's rather confusing story involving a daisy and a cell phone. She missed the simplicity of being a child, making up stories for her dolls, making sure they were happy.

But life wasn't dolls. And now more than ever she realized she couldn't make everyone happy. But what could she do? What was there for her to do?

The hymn "Trust and Obey" began playing in her head, but that answer seemed so trite. So pat. She doubted the hymn writer had ever been shot at.

She rubbed her thumb into her palm, seeing the bones in her knuckles. Weak. Powerless.

As the words formed in her head, she wondered if that was how Nathan felt. To a man used to being strong and capable, the two injuries he suffered would be frustrating. She was still angry at him, but she also began to understand him. She wished she had had the right words to say to him in the hospital when Shaun was shot, and now in the face of the news about Malaya. She should have been able to comfort him without preaching to him. He probably thought she was trying to shove Jesus down his throat.

Which was ironic since she hadn't felt very close to Jesus lately.

She should pray. Instead she sat there, listening to Charity with one ear and listening for Nathan's footstep with the other. How could she pray when she felt a million miles away from God? It seemed almost insulting for her to pray when anger still sizzled inside her at how God had allowed Malaya to die, when she felt so betrayed and abandoned by Him. God wouldn't want to hear from her now. He'd want to hear from her when she was calmer, more sure of herself and the next step to take, more trusting in God.

But then again, how would she become any of those things without praying?

Oh, God, please help us. What should I do? She bit her lip. *Tell me what to do. Give me wisdom.*

She felt like she'd done nothing more than spoken aloud to a bare, empty room.

ELEVEN

Nathan didn't find answers in the pine and redwood trees that lined the small clearing where the cabin stood. They whispered, but he couldn't understand what they said. At times, he felt they mocked him.

Why had he gotten so upset at her? Why had he let the situation frustrate him this way? He needed to use his head. He needed to stop hurting her. Why was he always hurting her?

Because he was broken, that's why. He shouldn't be around her. He was barely able to protect her. She shouldn't have come to him for help.

Well, it was too late now. He had to do his best for her and Charity. He wouldn't give up. He wouldn't stay out here and feel sorry for himself.

He went inside, suddenly noticing the darkness and the biting wind. His hand as he opened the heavy oak door was stiff and ice cold. The house seemed warm to him, but Arissa crouched in front of the fireplace with a blanket wrapped around her. She looked at him with relief as he came inside. "I tried to build up the fire, but I think I made it worse."

Yes, the blaze had damped to a fitful flickering. Nathan knelt in front while she joined Charity on the couch, where the little girl was curled up asleep under a mound of more blankets. "I should have come in sooner to take care of this," he said gruffly.

She didn't answer, which both relieved him and made him feel guilty at the same time.

Tending to the fire gave him an excuse not to look at her, which made it easier to say, "I'm sorry I got upset."

"I'm sorry, too," she said softly. But the mood between them was still stiff and awkward, cluttered with the words they'd flung at each other.

"I've been thinking about what we should do," Nathan said.

"There doesn't seem many options for us." She sounded gloomy.

"But there are some things we can still do." At least for now.

"What, look through Mark's papers again?" She gestured to the two boxes that they'd brought with them.

Nathan had been intensely relieved that he'd taken the boxes with him to Mr. Brummel's side of the duplex the night before the men trashed Liam's place, keeping the contents from the gang, but even he wasn't sure there was any more information there. "We never really looked into that other key on Mark's chain."

"But it's probably for an apartment, right?"

"Liam pointed out that the key looks new. It could be that the landlord just installed new locks, or that Mark rented a new one, or that Mark didn't have the key long enough for it to get dinged up. But I'm wondering if this isn't a key to an apartment. Maybe it's a key to a cabin like this that Mark bought for cheap."

"But we didn't see any large withdrawals from his bank account."

"He could have received money from the gang and paid in cash without depositing it."

She looked thoughtful. "True. I would think that if he did buy something like a cabin, he'd have bought other small things like supplies."

"We can check his credit card statements again."

Arissa sighed, but said, "Okay." She untangled herself from where she sat next to Charity's sleeping form and the two of them sat on a blanket on the floor and sifted through the paperwork again.

They concentrated on the credit card statements, this time looking for small purchases that might point to a second home Mark could have bought. "He wouldn't have bought something under his name, I suppose?" Arissa said.

"He probably paid cash, maybe under the table. Maybe using a fake name and ID."

"Why would he want to hide all this from the gang in the first place? He was a mole for them."

"It probably wasn't wise to let them know too much about his private business."

"And what was his private business? Why exactly was he in Sonoma?"

Nathan rubbed his eyes, which felt gritty. "Why would he have an account here rather than some other bank in Los Angeles?"

"Maybe the LSLs really are moving up north. Maybe Steve wasn't lying about that."

"Even if it were true, why would they need Mark here? He wasn't one of the captains and they needed him for his L.A. info."

Arissa chewed on her lip. "True. And it's starting to look like the gang didn't know anything about his movements up here."

"Plus the rumors are recent. Mark was up here in Sonoma three years ago."

"Moving a drug operation must take a long time. It could be that the LSLs started working on it three years ago."

Nathan wanted to retort that it would have been impossible to keep that a secret for three years, but then he wondered. If only the top-ranking captains knew about it, they could be the ones doing most of the logistical work to plan the move. And they were less likely to blab about what the gang was doing because it might cause repercussions with rival gangs. "Maybe."

"Mark had to have a specific reason for being in Sonoma," Arissa said. "But none of this tells us. He was so secretive, we'll probably never know."

They sat in silence, both of them disgruntled.

"What if…" Arissa swallowed. "What if we can't find anything? What then?"

He knew the answer, but he didn't speak for a long time because he was unwilling to voice it. But finally he said quietly, "Then you and Charity need to disappear."

The muscle at her throat flinched. She didn't meet his eyes, instead looking into the fire. "I suppose Liam can help us with that," she said in a flat voice.

"Yes." He felt hollow when he said it.

"I've never been alone before."

The despairing words hung in the air between them. Nathan didn't want her to be alone. A woman and child, staying under the radar, running maybe for the rest of their lives? Or until the gang caught up to them. He remembered, then, what he'd told Charity in the bank about not leaving them. He realized he didn't want to leave them.

He didn't want to leave them *unprotected,* that was all. Yes, that was it. "I'll go with you," he told her.

The glow in her eyes rivaled the fire. "Are you sure?"

"It's not safe for just the two of you. But ideally, we have to try to find out what the gang needs with Charity."

"I don't want to run, Nathan." She reached over to take his hand. "And what about my family? Your family?"

Her hand on his looked both delicate and strong. Fiercely loving, fiercely loyal. He turned his hand over to clasp hers. "I don't know."

"I don't want to run until we've exhausted absolutely every lead." Her voice had the hard edge of determination to it. "Mark may not have bought anything with a credit card in Sonoma, but he had to have talked to people."

"He talked to my parents."

"And he might have talked to my Aunt Luellen. My mother said Aunt Luellen never mentioned Mark visiting her, but it was three years ago. She might be mistaken."

"All right, we can go talk to them tomorrow."

Nathan didn't say it, yet they both knew that these were their last leads, and they weren't very strong. But the alternative was difficult to face.

His parents and her aunt were their last hope.

More than one head turned as Nathan, Arissa and Charity walked in through the front doors of the Sonoma Police Department. Nathan's skin prickled as he casually assessed everyone in the front room of the building, disliking the attention. Their entrance shouldn't have been noteworthy except that the shooting at Liam's house was probably not a common occurrence in a tiny tourist town, and most of these men and women grew up with both the O'Neills and Fischers.

"Hey, Nathan." Joseph Fong hurried toward them, a clipboard in his hand. "I didn't expect to see you here."

Nathan shook the younger man's outstretched hand.

"Hi, Arissa." Joseph's smile was a bit warmer as the turned to her, and he held her hand longer than strictly necessary. However, she seemed to find something about him unsettling, and extricated her hand with a tug.

"Nathan, Arissa." Another voice called to them and then Charlie Granger was at Joseph's elbow. "Hi, guys. Are you three all right after yesterday?"

"We're fine," Arissa told him with a smile.

"I'm sorry I didn't get there until late," Charlie said. "It was my turn to watch your parents' house, Nathan, so when I got the call to leave my post and respond, it took me a while to get to Liam's house."

"It was nice of you to notice me on the side of the road," Arissa said.

Charlie blushed. "Aw, you were already in good hands since Detective Carter had stopped to make sure you were okay."

"I wish I'd gotten there a second sooner," Joseph said. "I might have seen the two guys leaving." Joseph had been a bit overeager when he'd arrived at Liam's house. He'd been the first at the scene and squatted next to Nathan and Shaun. When Nathan told him he'd called the ambulance for Shaun, Joseph had asked where Arissa and Charity were and if they were all right.

After seeing the way he held Arissa's hand, Nathan wondered if his eagerness had more to do with Arissa than with being a good officer.

"Did you change your mind about police protection?" Joseph glanced at Arissa and Charity. "I'm still more than willing to be reassigned to you—"

"Sorry, Joseph, I just need to speak to Detective Carter in his office. Is he available?"

"Oh, sure. Let me get him." Joseph wandered back, his crew-cut head disappearing in the sea of other taller officers.

"I know Arissa's in good hands with you," Charlie said to Nathan, "but if you ever need us, just call me and Joseph and we'll come help you out."

"I appreciate that, Charlie."

"We're a bit busier now that we're not assigned to watching your parents' house." Charlie smiled sheepishly. "I have to admit that was kind of boring."

Joseph returned, panting slightly. "Detective Carter was on the phone, but he told me to bring you to him right away."

"We don't want to interrupt him," Arissa said.

"Naw, I think he was almost done." Joseph walked them toward the back of the building, guiding them through the officers milling around. "Did you guys find somewhere safe to hole up?"

"Joe, leave off." Charlie gave him a mild

punch to the arm. "They can't exactly tell you where."

"Just curious." But Joseph grinned at the other officer, then turned to give Arissa a wink. She stiffened at the familiarity, although she gave him a tight smile in return.

The exchange irritated Nathan. He told himself it was because there was the possibility that someone in Sonoma had tipped off the gang members about Liam's house. Had it been Joseph or Charlie? Or any of the officers here? They had access to databases and could have found Liam's name on the lease.

Joseph knocked on Detective Carter's door, which was ajar, and although he was behind his desk still on the phone, he waved them inside. In a few seconds, he'd hung up and dismissed the two officers. "Didn't realize you needed a full escort," he remarked with a twinkle in his gray eyes as Joseph and Charlie headed back to the front of the police station.

Color rose in Arissa's cheeks, but Nathan laughed it off. "I don't remember being that eager as a cadet."

"Well, Joseph's just out of the academy and sometimes he rubs off on Charlie, even though he had another career before joining the force. Sit down." He pointed to the two seats in front of his desk.

Nathan closed the office door. "I actually only wanted to call my parents from your phone, if you don't mind. It wouldn't look odd for you to call Roland Gibbs since you're friends."

Detective Carter's reddish eyebrows rose toward his receding hairline. "You take 'caution' to a whole new level, Fischer."

"Just call it paranoia, Detective." Nathan smiled. "Can I put it on speaker phone?"

"I'd appreciate that."

The detective punched a few buttons on his phone and then dialed retired detective Roland Gibbs's home. The phone only rang a couple times. "Gibbs," the gruff voice answered.

"It's Nathan Fischer."

"Oh, yes. Hang on."

A pause, then his mother's voice. "Nathan, are you all right?"

"I'm fine, Mom. How are you and Dad holding up?"

To his surprise, his mother gave a snort. "Your father is having a ball. He and Roland have gone fishing at the stream in his backyard every day and I've been dying of boredom. The man doesn't even have cable television."

Nathan bit back a smile. "Sorry about that, Mom."

"Please tell me this will be over soon."

Nathan sobered quickly. He wasn't sure what to tell her.

Detective Carter spoke up. "Mrs. Fischer, it's Detective Carter. I assure you we're doing everything we can to find those men who are after your son and discover what they're up to. I give you my word I won't rest until I have answers."

Nathan met the man's steely gaze with surprise and gratitude. He knew Detective Carter didn't give his promises lightly because he always followed through on them. It made Nathan feel a bit more at ease to know the man was standing beside him, despite the fact Nathan hadn't wanted police protection for the three of them.

"Thank you, Detective Carter," his mom said. "Nathan, are Arissa and Charity all right?"

"We're here, Kat," Arissa said. "We're fine, thanks to Nathan and Detective Carter watching over us."

"Oh good, I'm glad nothing bad has happened to you all," Mom said.

Nathan and Arissa shared a guilty look, but didn't update her. She didn't get much of the local news or gossip out at Roland Gibbs's ranch, which was all for the best.

"Did you need to talk to your father?" his mom asked.

"No, actually, we needed to talk to you, Mom."

"Me? Whatever for?"

"You mentioned seeing Mark in Sonoma," Arissa said. "Do you remember when you saw him?"

"Hmm…" Nathan could picture her rubbing her forehead with her palm, the way he knew he did when he was thinking. "It was so long ago. I'm not sure."

"How about the time of year of each time you saw him?" Arissa asked.

Good idea, Nathan thought. "How many times did you see him, Mom?"

"Let me see… The first time was I think in the grocery store. He was buying bagels—yes, I remember because I recommended the onion bagels. It was later in the day—he said he was staying with his aunt overnight and heading out early in the morning, so he was buying breakfast ahead of time."

He stayed with his aunt? Nathan raised his eyebrows at Arissa, who had also caught the mention about the overnight stay, and shook her head in confusion.

"I think he mentioned something about driving his aunt into downtown Sonoma for her to do her shopping."

Arissa nodded. "My aunt doesn't drive anymore. She usually gets one of her other friends to take her places."

"I'm afraid I don't remember the weather or the time of year."

"That's okay, Mom. How about the next time?"

"We were walking in the square. He was walking, too—he'd been shopping, I think, because he had a bag from the office supply store. He mentioned he had driven his aunt to Sonoma again—or maybe I asked him if that's what he did, and he agreed? I can't remember. Anyway, he said he'd been about to head back to L.A. but he had picked up a few supplies he needed, while he remembered, since the store was right there. That's when your father and I invited him to dinner. At first he said no, but we bullied him into accepting."

Arissa smiled at his mother's comment.

"Did you see what he'd bought?"

"No, I'm afraid I don't remember."

"What did you talk about at dinner?"

"Oh, I don't know that I remember that, either. Just little things, nothing important. We probably talked about you, Arissa, and your folks. And about Nathan. He didn't say anything that stood out to me or made me think something was wrong. He was always so full of energy, so charming."

Yes, he had been that. He and Nathan had both always been ready for action, always willing to do what needed to be done. And despite knowing Mark had been a mole, Nathan found himself missing his partner more than he ever had before. Maybe that meant he was finally letting the past go.

"I think that was summertime, because I remember it was very hot. We had the air conditioning running full blast and I made a cold zucchini soup. Mark asked for seconds of that."

Summer. Nathan tried to remember if Mark had been absent from work the summer before he died, but he couldn't remember anything out of the ordinary. Mark must have gone to Sonoma on his days off.

"We met him two other times that I can remember," his mom said, "but I don't remember which was first. Once was in Sonoma again, and once was in Santa Rosa."

"Where in Sonoma?"

"In that coffee shop off the square. He

was sitting at a table next to a window and just looking out. I teased him about stalking some girl, and he looked faintly guilty. That made me wonder if he was up in Sonoma because of a girlfriend."

After seeing his notes to Jemma and the ring, Nathan didn't think so. But maybe Mark *had* been stalking someone—or at least observing them. But who?

"We invited him to dinner then, too, but he said no, he had to get back to Los Angeles. I remember it was cold, so maybe it was fall or winter."

How many months had Mark been coming to Sonoma? Over a year? "How about that time in Santa Rosa, Mom?"

"That was during some cold month, too. Your father and I like that one Indian restaurant in Santa Rosa, do you remember the one? We had dinner and went walking to the gelato place a few stores down from the restaurant—not for gelato, it was too cold for that, but they make the most divine hot chocolate, it's thick like—"

"Mom?"

"Oops, sorry. Anyway, we literally bumped into Mark."

"Why was he in Santa Rosa?"

"He said his aunt's house was around the corner."

Arissa suddenly jerked in her seat. She moved so violently that Charity, sitting in her lap, started as well. Nathan looked at her, but she simply shook her head and waved her hand, indicating for him to continue talking to his mother.

"Do you remember what you talked about?"

"No, I'm sorry. We had hot chocolate together. I'm telling you, Nathan, he didn't say anything that made me curious or suspicious or that seemed odd."

Mark had had that way of relating to people that was completely guileless. Maybe that's why Nathan hadn't even suspected him of selling information to the LSLs until that day at the chop shop, when the news had been almost like a physical blow.

"Mark didn't mention anything else about our aunt Luellen, did he?" Arissa asked.

"Nothing that seemed strange. The overall

impression I got of her was that she was old and a bit set in her ways. She married your mother's brother, I think?"

"Yes, and then after he passed away, she remarried, so her last name isn't Filipino anymore, it's Delmore."

"Yes, now that you mention it, I remember that's what Mark told us. I guess her second husband passed away, too?"

"Yes, several years ago. She lives alone now."

"Mark said she was very independent."

Arissa chuckled. "That's a nice way of saying she's used to having her own way and wouldn't go live with any of her children."

"Well, any other questions for me?"

"Thanks for going over this with us, Kat," Arissa said.

"Thanks, Mom. Try to stay out of trouble, okay?" Nathan said.

"Detective Carter, I am charging you with bringing me some magazines in the next few days," his mother said sternly. "Otherwise, I might commit homicide if Robert tells me one more fishing tale…"

"I'll bring you those magazines tonight, how about that?" Detective Carter had an amused lilt to his voice.

"Thank you very much."

"Bye, Mom."

As soon as the detective disconnected the call and turned off the speakerphone, Nathan asked Arissa, "What was it?"

There was a triumphant gleam in her eye. "My Aunt Luellen lives in Cotati, not Santa Rosa."

Something bloomed inside of him, something exciting.

"She's never lived in Santa Rosa," Arissa continued. "And none of her kids lives in Santa Rosa. So what was Mark doing there, claiming he was staying close by?"

"Your mom said Mark hadn't visited your aunt, but maybe we need to talk to her anyway."

"Do you really think she'd know why Mark was in Santa Rosa, especially when it sounds like he never actually went to visit her?"

"At first we thought he used your aunt

Luellen as his excuse for being in Sonoma, but he could have said he's visiting an old school friend in Santa Rosa, or even invented some other girlfriend. But he mentioned your aunt." The wheels were turning in Nathan's head. He knew that the human brain worked in very predictable ways. "I think that he mentioned her because his business up here might have some association with her. Besides, what do we have to lose?"

It was a tenuous thread, but he'd take it.

He didn't know what else to do.

Arissa's Aunt Luellen's house on the outskirts of Cotati looked even more weather-beaten than the last time Arissa had seen it, which had been several years ago. Arissa's parents hadn't been able to leave the grocery store for vacations, but Mom called Aunt Luellen once every two weeks just to check on her, even though she was sort of an ex-sister-in-law.

The sky had become overcast, giving the faded white-washed boards a dingier cast. But Arissa noticed that the front yard didn't look as scraggly as she remembered. Chickens scattered in front of the SUV as Nathan pulled into the driveway, and the neighing of Aunt Luellen's goats sounded when Arissa exited of the car. She helped Charity out of the car, too. "You'll get to meet Aunt Luellen for the first time, won't that be fun?"

Charity just looked up at her with large dark eyes.

"She's the one who gave you that stuffed turtle at Christmas, remember? He lit up at night and made stars appear on the ceiling."

Charity's eyes brightened. "Mr. Green."

"Yes, Mr. Green." Unfortunately, the stuffed night-light animal was probably ripped to shreds in the ruins of her parents' apartment.

They approached the front door, which had a brand-new screen door, and rang the old-fashioned doorbell. It ding-donged inside, then a firm tread sounded coming to the door. It was flung open, and through the screen, the figure of a wiry Filipino man stood.

Nathan jerked backward in surprise, but Arissa shouted, "Uncle Lew!"

He pushed open the screen door, his face a mass of smile lines, and accepted his niece's hearty hug. "Arissa! Why didn't you say you were coming?"

"I forgot Aunt Luellen's phone number, and the trip was unexpected."

Nathan cleared his throat.

Arissa stepped back. "Uncle Lew, this is Nathan Fischer. He and Mark were friends. Nathan, this is Aunt Luellen's brother, my Uncle Lewis." He wasn't related by blood, but she'd always called him her uncle.

The two men shook hands.

"Uncle Lew, this is Charity." Since he'd been overseas for so long, he hadn't yet met her.

Charity hung back, but Uncle Lew knelt and smiled at her. "I'm your Uncle Lew. I sent you a stuffed turtle at Christmas, do you remember that?"

While Charity nodded warily, Arissa said, "You sent it? I thought it was from Aunt Luellen."

"It was, but I got it for her. She just wrapped it and sent it for the two of us." His sparkling dark eyes peered up at his niece-by-marriage. "I take it she only put her name?" He sighed and shook his head. "That's my sister for you."

"Charity loved—er, loves it, Uncle Lew. What are you doing here? I thought you were in Taiwan."

"I retired."

"You did? Mom didn't say anything about it."

"Luellen probably didn't tell her because she's mad at me for retiring. She liked the care packages of Chinese food I sent to her."

Yet another typical response from her atypical aunt. Arissa and Uncle Lew both rolled their eyes at the same time.

"Lew!" a voice shouted from inside the house. "Who's there?"

"You'd find out if you came out here!" he yelled back, not in the least cowed by his cantankerous sister. He turned to Arissa. "I'm tempted to have you stay here just to make her walk to the front door, but come on in."

They entered the narrow, low-ceilinged hallway paneled with oak. Last time Arissa had been here, the hallway had been crammed with small tables holding photo frames and figurines, but now it was clear and the photo frames were hung on the walls. "Did you hang these?" She touched a photo and looked at her uncle.

"Yep. Started fixing the place up. I'm going to let my apartment in Santa Rosa go and live with Luellen from now on."

"You're...you have an apartment in Santa Rosa?" Arissa stopped in her tracks. "Since when?"

"I bought it a few years ago when the housing market first dipped, even though I knew I wouldn't stay there much." He explained to Nathan, "I worked for an international export company that based me out of Taiwan, so I only came to the U.S. once every six weeks, and I only stayed for two weeks at a time. I used to stay with Luellen, but since I had the money, and the Santa Rosa apartment was pretty new and going for cheap..." He shrugged.

Nathan opened his mouth to ask a question, but he was interrupted by Aunt Luellen's roar, "Lew! What are you dawdling for?"

"I'll take my time, you old bat," he returned, and led them to the end of the hallway and into the living room. The morning light filtered through the large sliding glass door facing the backyard, where two of Aunt Luellen's goats were eating.

A ratty recliner sat in front of an impressive HD flat-screen television that seemed out of place in the room, with its old, worn furniture cluttered with baskets holding cleaned mohair from the goats, ready to be carded. Arissa remembered summers where she and Mark had been forced by Aunt Luellen to help her prepare the scoured fiber for spinning, which Aunt Luellen sold to a local dyer.

In the recliner sat her diminutive Aunt Luellen, who stopped in the act of spinning some of her carded fiber at a spinning wheel.

She looked sweetly domestic, but the fierce glare she shot at Arissa could have curdled milk. "So you finally come visit, huh? I wondered if you'd dropped off the planet."

"Hi, Aunt Luellen." Arissa dropped a kiss on her cheek, then gently pushed a very reluctant Charity forward. "This is Charity."

At sight of the child, Luellen's dark eyes softened. "Mark's kid, huh?" Her tone had softened, too. "She looks like him." Then she raised her eyes to Nathan, and they returned to shooting daggers. "Who are you?"

"Mark's old partner in the LAPD," he hastened to say. "Nathan Fischer."

Aunt Luellen gestured to Nathan with a movement of her iron-gray head. "Your boyfriend?" she said to Arissa.

"No," Arissa replied, unfazed. Arissa's single status was usually among the first things Aunt Luellen commented on when she and Arissa's mom talked.

"Well then, why's he here? And stop standing around, find someplace to sit."

Uncle Lew had been grabbing baskets of fiber and moving them around the room to clear off the ancient sofa for them. When Arissa sank down, she found the cushion so thin that it was almost nonexistent.

She turned to Aunt Luellen. "We found some keys that belonged to Mark." She looked to Nathan, who dug the keys out of his pocket and held them up. "One is for a safe deposit box in Sonoma, but the other looks like a house or apartment key. Since you're our only relative who lives in Nor-Cal, we wondered if he had told you anything about it." She already had a feeling she knew the answer.

"No, he didn't say anything to me." Aunt Luellen frowned, as if insulted Mark hadn't confided in her.

But Uncle Lew stared at the key. "Might be mine."

"Yours?" Aunt Luellen rounded on him. "Why would Mark have your apartment key? And why wouldn't he tell me about it?"

Uncle Lew gave her a dry look. "You really think he'd bother to tell you about it? He came directly to me."

Arissa hadn't know her brother was that

close to their uncle. "He came to you for what?"

"He called my cell phone—I guess he figured I was in Taiwan, but I happened to be at my apartment at the time. He originally wanted to know if he could leave some things in my storage unit. When I asked him about it, he said he had a girlfriend up in Sonoma that he visited every so often, and since he was staying in hotel rooms, he wanted a place for extra clothes. Well, I told him he could bunk at my apartment. I have a guest room I don't use."

"A girlfriend?" Aunt Luellen looked insulted. "How could he not say anything about that to me? Or to his mother?"

Uncle Lew raised an eyebrow at her. "He said he didn't want anybody knowing about his girlfriend, including his parents."

Aunt Luellen still looked peeved.

"Did he say who his girlfriend was?"

"No, and I respected his privacy. After living with Luellen for this long, I learned to value it."

"Hey!" she protested.

Uncle Lew just gave her a cheeky grin.

But Arissa could understand how Uncle Lew would have kept her brother's secret. Her uncle wasn't intimidated by his sister and he disapproved of her nosiness, so out of his own sense of privacy, he'd have allowed Mark his own secrets. Also, he hardly ever spoke to Arissa's mom. He wouldn't have had a chance to tell her after Mark's death, and he certainly wouldn't have told Aunt Luellen, ever.

"What did you do with Mark's things after he died?" Nathan's voice had an anxious edge to it.

"Since I wasn't in my apartment very often, I left them in the guest room for almost a year. Then I just boxed everything up and put it in the garage. I know I ought to have given it to your mom, Arissa, but after I stuck everything in the garage, I forgot about it."

A nervous electricity raced through her arms. "Can we see it, Uncle Lew? We think there's something there to do with Charity."

"Sure." He rose to his feet. "I can take you now."

"They barely got here," Aunt Luellen protested.

"They might come back to see you," Uncle Lew said carelessly over his shoulder as he exited the living room.

"Thanks for everything, Aunt Luellen." Arissa hastily kissed her aunt's cheek and took Charity by the hand. "Say goodbye, Charity."

"Bye."

Aunt Luellen reached out a gnarled hand to finger the girl's cheek. "You look just like your daddy," she said gruffly.

"Goodbye, Mrs. Delmore," Nathan said.

They met Uncle Lew outside where he stood by the SUV. "You drive," he said to Nathan.

He led them to a small section of Santa Rosa with several newish condos covering a couple blocks next to a tiny park. He had them pull in a driveway in front of a closed garage door.

"Uncle Lew, this is a condo, not an apartment."

"Condo, apartment, what's the difference?" He led them up a flight of stairs alongside the garage to the front door. It looked like the garage was the first floor, and then the condo itself was two floors.

He breathed heavily as he unlocked his door. "Another reason why I'm going to live with your aunt," he said to Arissa. "Getting too old for the stairs. Plus she's getting on, too."

They entered into his living room, a small space that was rather bare, which Arissa would expect since Uncle Lew was rarely home. There was a nice television in the living room and a comfortable-looking leather recliner, and then one other wooden chair, but no sofa. The kitchen connected to the living room, and its counters were empty except for a microwave and a toaster. A flight of stairs led to the bedrooms above, but Uncle Lew took them to a door that looked like a coat closet, but proved to be a flight of stairs heading down to the garage.

The dark area was piled with boxes, mostly. "Sorry for the mess," Uncle Lew said as he flicked on the light and kicked at some boxes to shove them aside so they could walk further. He walked to two small boxes in the corner. "These are Mark's."

Nathan picked up one box and Arissa got the other one. They went back to the living room, but Uncle Lew said, "Why don't you two go to one of the bedrooms to look through those? Charity and I will watch TV here."

Arissa was surprised at his suggestion, but he continued, "I know you didn't come all the way to NorCal just to ask your gorgon aunt about any old keys. Mark was in trouble, wasn't he?"

Arissa gave him a sad look, but didn't answer.

He patted her shoulder with an awkward, heavy hand. "When he came to me, I didn't want to pry, but I wondered, even though his story about the girlfriend seemed legit. You're not in trouble, are you?"

"Probably the less we say to you, the better," Nathan said.

Uncle Lew shook his head, then his eye fell on Charity. "When I was packing up Mark's things to put them in the garage, I came across a stuffed turtle."

"Mr. Green," Charity suddenly said.

Uncle Lew smiled, and his face became a mass of wrinkles again. "Is that his name? He looked like a Mr. Green to me, too. Anyway," he said to Arissa, "I packed it in his boxes and forgot about it. But a few months ago, when Luellen told me about you adopting Mark's daughter, I guessed he'd bought it for her. That's why I dug it out and gave the turtle to Luellen to send to Charity for Christmas. I didn't feel comfortable telling your mom where I got it from."

Tears prickled in Arissa's eyes. Mark had bought it for his unborn daughter, and it had eventually made its way to her. "Thanks, Uncle Lew."

"No problem," he said gruffly. He motioned up the stairs. "Go on up."

They quickly found the guest bedroom and

set down the boxes. The room had a queen-size bed, a dresser and a bedside table, but nothing else. The closet only contained some hangers.

Arissa shut the drawer of the bedside table. "I guess I was hoping to still find something of Mark's in here."

"It was worth a try," Nathan said. "Let's look in these boxes."

It took only ten minutes for Arissa to realize what Mark had been up to. Her heart beat faster as she flipped through more pages. Then she found the name and phone number scribbled on a pad of paper: Doug T. Johnson, FBI.

"He was collecting evidence against the LSL gang," she breathed. "He was going to turn it in to the FBI."

Nathan sat back, his face slack as he stared at the blank wall. "He was working against the LSLs."

But not always. He had, indeed, been a mole for the LSLs, apparently for the money to pay off their mom's medical bills. But then seven months before his death, he started collecting evidence that the FBI could use in an investigation to solidly prosecute the top officials in the gang, cutting off the dragon's head.

"It looks like he intended to give this to the FBI, then take Charity and Jemma and go into witness protection." Nathan passed some papers to Arissa.

"He started doing this when he found out Jemma was pregnant," Arissa said.

"This still doesn't explain why the gang needs Charity."

They discovered that within minutes. "Nathan." Arissa showed him some documents she'd discovered. "This looks like a police document."

He scanned it. "This is three million dollars in cash seized from an LSL drug house about six months before Mark died. It's in the evidence locker... Wait a minute." He read the next page.

"It's not in the evidence locker." Arissa handed him the papers she'd just found. "It's in an offshore bank account, owned by Mark."

Nathan looked closely at the sheet in his hand. "This is a copy of an email. Mark was tasked by the LSLs to get the money out of the evidence locker and return it to them. But it looks like after he got the money out, he never gave it to the gang."

"But the gang wouldn't let him get away with that. They'd notice if he never showed up with the money he was supposed to give to them."

"Wait, I remember seeing something." Nathan sifted through some papers on the bed beside him. "Here. I didn't understand it at first, but now I think I do. Mark paid someone to hack in and doctor the gang's accounting program and bank account so they wouldn't notice the money wasn't there."

Suddenly the pieces fell into place. "The move north. If the gang really is moving, they have to move their money, too. And they'd finally notice they're missing three million dollars. That's why they're only after Charity now, three years after Mark's death."

They continued going through the papers,

and Nathan said, "Arissa, I know why they had to take both you and Charity."

She saw a thick, legal-looking document in his hand.

"I don't know if I entirely understand this," Nathan said, "but for Mark's offshore bank account, he stipulated that only Charity can access it, and she has to be either of age or accompanied by her parents. Since they're both dead, by her legal guardian."

"The LSLs need both of us to get back their three million dollars."

"And this contract requires a DNA test, so the child and guardian retrieving the money have to be related to Mark by blood. None of Charity's mother's family can access the account."

"That explains it. I wonder if they already flew to the bank and tried to access it with a fake child and guardian? They would have discovered about the DNA stipulation."

"Even if they don't know that Charity's mother's family aren't allowed access to the account, you're her legal guardian. It's on public record. If they had Charity, they couldn't access the account without you."

"This was his nest egg. When he went into witness protection with his family, he'd have this money, unknown to the FBI."

"And if the gang found out about the stolen money, he'd be long gone."

"How'd the gang know it was Mark who stole the money?"

"They probably tortured the info out of the accountant who hacked in and doctored the records."

A shiver passed through her. Yes, that sounded like the LSL gang. "Nathan, what do we do? We can't give them the money, but if we don't…we're dead."

TWELVE

Nathan had thought he'd have a surer plan once he found out what Mark had done. Instead, it just opened up a dark pit that they couldn't escape from.

He drove toward the cabin in the fading light of the afternoon, but even the bouncing of the uneven dirt track couldn't distract him from the questions circling in his mind. What was the best thing for them to do?

They had soon discovered that, although he'd collected a lot, Mark hadn't amassed enough evidence for the FBI to solidly prosecute the LSL gang leaders. If any of them escaped conviction, the gang would live on and take out Arissa and Charity in revenge for Mark stealing the money. They had to turn the money in to the authorities, but it would anger the gang. Arissa and Charity would be unprotected and in danger.

He didn't know what to do.

He turned the bend in the road and the cabin flashed into view through the trees. Maybe he just needed to sleep on it and the answer would come in the morning.

As he climbed out of the vehicle, Charlie Granger appeared from around the corner of the cabin.

With his gun pointed straight at them.

"Hands up, Nathan." His voice was still the same pleasant voice he'd always had, but now with a slight edge to it. "Throw your weapon on the ground and kick it to me."

He unholstered his Glock and did as Charlie said.

"Your reserve weapon, too."

"I don't—"

Charlie fired and the bullet shattered the front window of the car. Charity shrieked and began to cry.

Nathan dug his smaller pistol out of his ankle holster and kicked it toward Charlie. "How'd you find us?"

"It was a lot harder than finding Liam's place. That only took a little time because I didn't know Liam was back in Sonoma until my mom bumped into Brady's wife at the grocery store a couple days ago."

Nathan ground his teeth, but tried to will himself to calm down. He opened his mouth to ask another question, keep him talking, but then Charlie darted in and grabbed Charity from Arissa's grasp.

"Charity!"

"Stay back!" Charlie motioned with his gun.

Tears began to fall from Arissa's eyes. "This cabin was supposed to be safe."

"It would have been if my mom hadn't found out at church that Monica Grant is dating Shaun O'Neill. You know how those ladies love to talk about the families in town."

"This cabin isn't even in the Grants' name." Nathan took a step but made it look as if he was just shifting his weight.

"Do you really think it was that hard to talk to those ladies and find out about Becca Itoh's family?"

"You must be clever to have figured this all out." Arissa's voice sounded strange to Nathan's ears, even clouded by her crying.

Charlie's eyes narrowed. "Nice try, babe. Flattery isn't going to make me suddenly change my mind. Get in the car or I shoot the girl."

"No, you won't." Arissa's eyes had also narrowed. "You kill her, the LSLs never get their money."

Charlie's mouth tightened as Arissa called his bluff. He pointed the gun at Arissa, and Nathan's heart slammed into high gear. "I can still shoot you."

"You need me because I'm Charity's legal guardian. Charity can't access the money without me."

Doubt flashed briefly across Charlie's eyes. Nathan moved a step closer to him.

Arissa continued, not looking at Nathan, holding Charlie's attention. "If I die, Charity becomes a ward of the state. They appoint a new guardian, and if that guardian isn't a blood relation of Mark's, the bank won't allow her access to the account."

Nathan wasn't sure if all that about being a ward of the state was true, but Charlie apparently believed her. He realized his threat wasn't giving him as much of an advantage as he thought, and the tip of the gun wavered a fraction of an inch.

"Arissa, duck!" he shouted.

Arissa dropped to the ground.

Nathan tackled Charlie, and the two of them went down with Charity smashed between them and the ground. Hard earth bit into his elbow and slippery grass made his feet slide under him as he landed a punch to Charlie's face.

But Charlie didn't have a glass jaw like the LSL members in the storage unit. He was dazed for barely a second before he retaliated with an elbow at Nathan's temple.

Nathan twisted but got part of the blow. Still, it was enough time for Charlie to grab at the gun where it had dropped into the grass only a few inches away.

For a moment Nathan met Charlie's wide eyes over the barrel of the gun. His breath caught, but he realized Charlie hadn't fired.

He had mentored Charlie. Their families had grown up together. Nathan had one chance. "You're not a killer, Charlie."

Charlie froze for a moment that seemed like minutes, then his mouth pulled into a tight line, and he glanced down.

Too late, Nathan realized what he was going to do. Before he could roll off Charlie, the younger man slammed the butt of the gun into Nathan's injured thigh.

The blow wouldn't have been so painful if he hadn't still been recovering from the attack by the LSL gang member from only a couple days before. As soon as Charlie hit him, Nathan was engulfed by pain that shot stars in front of his eyes, and the edges of his vision began to fade. No, he had to stay conscious. He fought to clear his muddled head, but his body wouldn't respond to him. He dimly heard Charity and Arissa crying and screaming. Nathan managed to roll over, and from his vantage point near the ground he saw their legs under the edge of the open rear door of the car.

Then he saw it. His Glock, in the grass where he'd kicked it closer to Charlie.

Charity's tiny feet disappeared as Charlie pushed her into the car, but Arissa began fighting him. She kicked at him, and the two of them were obviously struggling.

Nathan's hand closed over the Glock. He had to make sure he aimed well. He didn't want to hit Arissa.

God, please help me.

The prayer bubbled up from the depths of his soul. He felt rusty, but the words seemed to cover his hand and steady it as he aimed and shot.

The bullet hit Charlie squarely in the calf.

He roared. Blood droplets splayed. Arissa's feet were suddenly flung away as if Charlie had pushed her down and away. Nathan tried to get to his feet, but the pain still radiated from his thigh, making his entire leg useless. Charlie closed the back door, then opened the passenger-side door. His feet disappeared as he launched himself into the SUV.

No, he was getting away! Nathan gave an animal cry as he forced himself to his feet, his leg on fire. Charlie's head was a dark blur moving from the passenger side to the driver's side behind the bullet-shattered front windshield.

Nathan fired at one of the front tires and missed. Charlie started the engine and threw it into gear.

"Nathan!"

Suddenly Arissa grabbed his arm and yanked him out of the way as Charlie gunned the car forward, hitting the wall of the cabin with the front bumper. Nathan and Arissa fell into the grass together, the impact jarring his leg.

They could only watch as the SUV backed up and shot out of the clearing with a spray of dirt from the back wheels.

Charity was gone.

Arissa felt as if she was clinging to the edge of a cliff, fingers clutching the bare rock, nothing but open space beneath her dangling feet. She was utterly helpless, utterly alone.

She sat curled up in the chair in Detective

Carter's office, her face buried in tissues because she didn't want to face the world, face reality.

Charity was gone. Her darling, precious niece was gone.

She felt as if the girl had been ripped out of her soul rather than ripped out of her arms. She'd seen Nathan stealthily move toward Charlie, had done her best to distract him, but it hadn't been enough. She hadn't done enough.

But what else could she have done?

She was so tired of trying to keep it together, trying to rein in her emotions, trying to focus her energies on what she could do. She was too weak to try, and her desperation washed over her.

Words sounded around her from Nathan, speaking to Detective Carter and the other officers. But all Arissa could think about was lying on the ground, watching Charity being taken away.

Then a snatch of Bible verse came to her: *He lifted me out of the slimy pit, out of the mud and mire.*

She did feel as though she'd been dropped into a muddy pit, and a part of her wanted to stay there, to wallow in her despair.

But then in her mind's eye she reached for the hand held out to her. It had her in a firm grip. It wouldn't let her fall.

She wiped at her eyes, reached for another tissue from the box on Detective Carter's desk and saw the worn Bible sitting on the edge of it. And she knew, somehow, it had been placed there just for her.

She picked it up, thumbed through it. She remembered the verse because she'd read it recently. She was going through Psalms with her discipler. It didn't take her long to find the full verses:

He lifted me out of the slimy pit, out of the mud and mire; he set my feet on a rock and gave me a firm place to stand. He put a new song in my mouth, a hymn of praise to our God. Many will see and fear and put their trust in the Lord.

The last words were like a spear thrust into her heart. *Trust in the Lord.* In all her anxiety and urgency, in all her fear and confusion, not once had she stopped to think that all her efforts were just that—*hers*. Not God's efforts.

Because somehow she hadn't trusted God to take care of her. She had kept thinking of more things she could do, almost as if she hadn't thought God could do anything for them.

Oh, God, forgive me.

She sat there weeping, but a different sort of crying from what she'd been doing before. This was a crying that came up from the depths of her soul, calling out to God in a wordless entreaty she didn't fully understand herself.

And when she was finished, she felt tired but also covered with peace like a heavy quilt. God was with her, and with Charity. She didn't know what He would do, but she knew she needed to trust Him.

Detective Carter's phone rang suddenly, and Arissa had a feeling she knew who the caller was.

"Carter," the detective answered, but then his gray eyes sharpened to deadly steel.

He didn't speak for a few seconds, then he opened his mouth, but was cut off. He put the handset back in the cradle with a grimness to his lips that spoke of tightly controlled anger.

"He wants to trade Charity for one hundred thousand dollars."

"It's a trap," Arissa and Nathan said at the same time.

A ghost of a smile appeared on Detective Carter's face as he glanced between the two of them. "I figured that one out myself, thanks."

"When?" Nathan asked. "And where?"

"Three hours at a cherry orchard outside Sonoma."

Arissa was confused. "That doesn't make sense. You could range officers behind the trees all around him—"

"No, the cherry tree trunks aren't wide enough to hide anyone," Detective Carter said. "It will be almost as open as a field."

"Did he mention Arissa?" Nathan asked.

"No, but he's probably guessing she would want to be there to see Charity."

"He needs me." Arissa sat up straighter. "He can't go back to the gang without me. Let me be bait."

"No," Detective Carter said firmly.

"Absolutely not," Nathan retorted with some heat.

"I can't get officers close enough to cover you," the detective said.

"You won't need to," Arissa said. "I'll have Nathan with me."

Nathan frowned at her. "What makes you think Charlie will agree to that?"

"Because he knows you're injured in your arm and especially your thigh. We can dress up your leg, you can limp more dramatically. Maybe we can get you a cane." She stared into his eyes, willing him to understand. "He'll underestimate you. He probably already does because of the blow he gave you at the cabin."

Some of the muscles in Nathan's face flinched at her words, but she knew that this was their only chance. "You're overestimating me," he said in a low, hard voice.

"No, I'm not." She grabbed his shoulders

and gave him a slight shake. "I know you can protect me. But we can deceive Charlie into thinking you can't." She turned to Detective Carter. "Can you think of a better solution?"

He eyed both of them, and it was obvious he didn't like her suggestion one bit, but he didn't have much choice. "Fine," he snapped. "You two wait here." The detective left and shut the office door behind him.

Nathan turned away from her, but she reached out and forced him to look at her. "Please, Nathan, I need you to understand."

"I do understand." He spoke through gritted teeth. "I just didn't expect you to rub my injury in my face like that."

"I'm sorry, I didn't mean to do that." Normally she would never have come up with a plan like this, never have spoken to Nathan about his leg, but this was Charity's life at stake. She wet her lips. "Despite what you feel about your injury, you're wrong to think you know how *I* feel about it." About him.

"Then you're being stupid," he shot back.

"I haven't been able to protect you very well."

"Yes, you have. Every time we've been attacked, you've fought for us, you've taken a bullet for us, you haven't ever given up. You would never abandon us." Her voice caught on those last words. Nathan was nothing like any of the other boyfriends she'd had. They had run at the first sign of trouble, but he had only clung to them harder. "I know you would have been willing to die for us, Nathan."

Tears had glassed over her eyes so she couldn't see his face clearly, but she felt the weight of his stare. The anger had drained out of him, but she couldn't quite read his expression.

"Nathan." She reached up and cupped his cheek in her hand.

He didn't move away from her—he grew very, very still.

"I am willing to do this because I know you'll protect me. I trust you *completely.*" And then she leaned forward and kissed him.

He didn't respond at first, but she tried to

convey everything she couldn't yet say to him, all that was in her heart. She trusted this wonderful, honorable man—and she wanted him to trust himself, too.

And then suddenly, fiercely, his arms went around her and he kissed her. She felt the strength of his arms and the tenderness of his mouth.

She kissed him as if she'd never let him go. As if she'd never kiss him again.

Nathan couldn't understand why she trusted him. But it felt like an energy drink sizzling in his veins.

He stood beside her in the middle of the cherry orchard, the leaves rustling above them in a night wind that brought the scent of cherry blossoms. He rested his hand against the trunk of a nearby tree, as if he needed it to help him stand, while his other hand clutched a cane.

His head still reeled from her kiss, which had ended only when Detective Carter came back into his office. But she'd spoken to him in words he'd been able to hear.

She trusted him. She didn't see a cripple. She didn't think his injury made him too broken. She didn't let his insecurities push her away.

She wanted him. To her, he wasn't half a man.

He'd been fighting a black mood ever since Charlie had driven away with Charity. He had trusted Charlie, had trusted in their past together. He had begun to realize that maybe Arissa had been right. He had been blaming God, but in this, he had no one to blame but himself.

And then she'd said those three words: *I trust you.* They had released something in him like a dam breaking. He'd pulled her close and returned her kiss, his emotions raging out of his swollen heart.

And he had vowed, then and there, that he'd die for her if he had to.

A flash of headlights made Arissa straighten. She glanced down at the duffel bag at his feet, filled with fake cash, only the top stacks of bills being real.

Charlie parked the car at the edge of the orchard and approached them, limping badly. The car's headlights illuminated them all and kept his figure in shadows until he drew closer, towing a crying Charity. She saw Arissa and tried to run to her, but Charlie held her wrist in a tight grip.

Nathan had thought at first the officer helping him had padded his leg with too many bandages, but apparently not, because as Charlie drew near, his lip curled as he took in Nathan's serious *injury.* "Bring me the bag," Charlie said to Arissa.

Nathan picked up the duffel bag, and Charlie snapped, "Not you."

"I can't carry the bag," Arissa said. "It's too heavy." Her voice was just the right mix of anxious trembling and sobbing worry.

Charlie's lip curled again, and he motioned Nathan forward, a few steps behind Arissa. Nathan made sure to exaggerate his limp.

Nathan hadn't clearly seen the gun in Charlie's other hand until he drew nearer, but he knew it had to have been there. Arissa's gaze fell on the weapon as well, and she looked at Nathan with a speaking glance.

Charlie wouldn't shoot her or Charity. It was both Nathan's advantage and also his point of weakness, because Charlie *could* shoot him.

As Arissa approached, Charity began wildly struggling against Charlie's grip on her wrist. The tip of his gun fell.

Nathan dropped the cane and whipped out his firearm that had been hidden beneath the bandages on his leg. "Freeze!"

Arissa darted forward and grabbed at Charity to pull her from Charlie.

At Nathan's words, shouts sounded and officers began swarming into the orchard from where they'd been hiding on their bellies in the neighboring vineyard, out of sight in the darkness.

Startled by Nathan's gun and the approaching officers, Charlie loosened his hold on Charity and she pulled free. But he recovered too quickly and lashed out, and his weapon smacked Arissa hard in the temple. She dropped to the ground.

"Arissa!" Nathan fired near Charlie's foot—the injured one—and he hobbled backward, hissing in pain with the movement.

Charity hesitated near Arissa, tugging at her hand, but Nathan called sharply, "Charity!"

The command in his voice made her look up, eyes wide and red from tears. Nathan gestured to her to come to him, and she hesitated only a moment before running to him, eluding Charlie's grasp as he recovered from the surprise of Nathan's shot and grabbed for the girl.

Charity's small arms wrapped tightly around his leg, and he touched her back once before firming his grip on the gun pointed at Charlie. "Drop your weapon."

Arissa moaned and began rising to her feet, and then Charlie reached down to grab her, forcing her in front of him as a shield.

Arissa. The sight of her with Charlie paralyzed Nathan. He might as well not even have a weapon, because Charlie had Arissa.

Mark had died in front of his eyes. Now Arissa would, too.

Oh, God. Oh, God.

"I dare you!" Charlie shouted to Nathan. "You won't do it. You won't shoot her."

Arissa shook her head, shaking off the effects of the blow to her temple and starting to understand what was going on. Charlie had his left arm wrapped around her throat, his other hand pointing the gun at Nathan.

It was dark. He wasn't confident he'd be able to hit the corrupt officer without hitting Arissa.

What could he do? What was there for him to do?

Arissa's voice sounded in his memory. *I trust you.*

Except it wasn't Arissa speaking to Nathan, suddenly it was Nathan speaking to God. *Lord, I trust You.*

He had nothing else he could do. His heart cried out within him, giving Jesus everything he had left. He was utterly, completely dependent upon God.

And then suddenly he could almost feel a soft touch on his head, on his hand. And he no longer felt alone.

More alert now, Arissa's eyes found Nathan's, wide but determined. She silently mouthed a word to him.

Prudence.

He didn't have time to object. She raised

her hand to her chest, where Charlie couldn't see, three fingers showing. She counted down: three, two, one.

God, help us, he prayed.

She was shorter than Charlie, so she didn't have a good angle to hit him in the jaw, but her elbow flew back and connected solidly below the ribs. He grunted and his hold on her slackened.

Then she dive-bombed to the ground, leaving Charlie's upper body exposed.

Nathan took aim and fired. The bullet hit Charlie squarely in the right shoulder, making him drop his gun. Within seconds, the nearest officers had grabbed him and Charlie was handcuffed.

Nathan's arms had turned to rubber, and he lowered his weapon.

Then Arissa flung herself into his arms, her cry of relief vibrating against his lips. He held her close, feeling Charity sandwiched between them, Arissa's heart beating against his chest in tune with his.

He was whole.

THIRTEEN

God couldn't have created a more perfect moon.

Arissa soaked in the soft light, a gentle summer evening breeze ruffling her hair and bringing the scent of peaches from the nearby orchard. Sitting beside her on the picnic blanket, Nathan poured more icy lemonade into her cup. It was full dark but the heat still wrapped around them like a blanket. Arissa took her cup and held it to her throat to cool her skin.

"So when do your parents start work in the boutique?" Nathan asked her.

"Monica talked to her father, and he says the Joy Luck Life Hotel and Spa is set to open in two months." Monica's father, Augustus Grant, had graciously offered the management job to her parents, allowing them to sell their grocery store and move to Sonoma. Arissa laughed. "Since there's a short break between them closing the store and starting work at the boutique, Dad said he wants to surprise Mom with a vacation to Hawaii. He asked me to get them tickets."

"Did you already put in your transfer to SFO?" Nathan asked.

"Yes, I'll start flying out of San Francisco in three weeks, maybe sooner." She looked out at the rolling foothills before them, striped with rows of grapevines that looked like blurry dark lines in the moonlight. Nathan had spread the picnic blanket on a patch of ground that overlooked the fields, with the moon hung like an ornament low in the sky above the horizon.

Nathan's breath tickled her ear as he leaned close to her, pressing a kiss at the pulse on her neck. "I feel like I haven't spent time with you in months."

"It's only been a couple weeks." Their moonlit dinner date had been exactly what she wanted—romantic and yet quiet, enabling them to talk or be silent and drink in the scenery.

"I almost forgot to tell you." Nathan took her empty plate from her lap. "Detective Carter called me today. The accountant is going to testify."

She breathed a deep sigh. Charlie had found out about the money Mark had stolen because he'd been an accountant before becoming a police officer, and one of his colleagues had been the accountant who had hacked in and doctored the gang's bank accounts for Mark. Charlie had told the gang, who had indeed tried to get into the account with a girl posing as Charity, only to discover they needed both Charity and Arissa to get their money back. After being arrested, Charlie had given up the name of the hacker. Combined with the information Mark had gathered, the accountant's testimony would be enough to destroy the gang's infrastructure. Soon they would never be a threat again.

"Without their leaders, there's no chance

the gang will go through with their plans to move to NorCal?" Arissa asked.

"Steve said that the LAPD doesn't think there are any remaining gang members who command the respect needed to organize them that way, and none of the junior officers knew much about the move plans."

"So we're safe. At last."

Nathan's head blotted out the moon and his lips were on hers, warm and tender. This was the man she remembered from before Mark was killed. Romantic and creative, planning a dinner like this, with a heart that would cherish her as if she were the only woman in the world.

He drew away from her a fraction of an inch, and his lips touched hers as he said, "I love you."

The words hung like bells in the air, bells that rang in her chest. "I love you," she said.

He grabbed her hand and kissed her knuckles. "I owe so much to you."

"No, Nathan, I owe my life to you."

"I would still be that hollow, burned-out shell if you hadn't come to me that night with Charity." She couldn't quite see his eyes, but they glittered in his shadowed face.

"I came to you because I trusted you," she replied.

Then her left hand, the one still held in his, felt something cool slip onto her ring finger. She started in surprise, something golden and joyful bubbling up inside her.

He kissed her again. "Will you marry me?"

"Oh, yes!" She threw her arms around his neck.

The solitaire diamond glittered on her hand, but brighter still was that perfect moon. Its soft light showered on them and Arissa felt joy, peace and love—from the God who watched over them, and the man holding her close to his heart.

* * * * *

Dear Reader,

Thank you for joining me once again for this trip to Sonoma, California! This tourist spot is still a small community at heart, which ends up increasing the danger to my hero and heroine, Nathan and Arissa.

When I wrote *Stalker in the Shadows*, Nathan Fischer simply appeared out of nowhere, it seemed, and I suddenly wanted to know more about this former narcotics detective with the wounded leg and sorrowful eyes. I hope you've enjoyed this story here as much as I did in writing it.

I love to hear from readers. You can email me at camy@camytang.com or write to me at P.O. Box 23143, San Jose, CA 95123-3134. I blog about knitting, my dog, knitting, tea, knitting, my husband's coffee fixation, food—oh, and did I mention my knitting obsession?—at http://camys-loft.blogspot.com/. I hope to see you all there!

Camy Tang

Questions for Discussion

1. Arissa suddenly finds herself and her family responsible for a three-year-old girl, the daughter of her deceased brother. Have you ever had a responsibility suddenly thrust upon you? How did it make you feel? What did you do about it?

2. Nathan is dealing with a painful episode in his past, and it has turned into a bitter inner wound. Can you relate to his pain? What should his friends and family have done for him? What should he have done for himself?

3. Arissa and Charity are threatened by a dangerous Filipino gang, who want them for reasons they don't know. Can you understand why she did what she did? What could she have done better?

4. Because of his bitterness, Nathan feels emotionally cut off from his family and friends. Can you relate to how he feels?

If he were your friend, what would you say to him?

5. Nathan's mother is a strong Christian who is comfortable speaking about her faith. Can you relate to her or do you know someone like her? What is your own way of sharing your faith?

6. Arissa used to be a party girl, but when she accepts Christ, her behavior changed dramatically. Did you experience something like this or do you know someone whose behavior changed once they came to know Christ?

7. Arissa keeps doing all she can to try to protect Charity, but she feels helpless and guilty for the trouble she brings to the people who have helped her. Have you been in a situation where things were completely out of your control and it seemed to be going from bad to worse? How did you feel? What did you do?

8. Nathan, a Christian for all his life, is upset at God because he can't under-

stand why God would allow the bullet to shatter his leg and cut short his career in the Los Angeles Police Department. Have you been in a situation where you question why God allowed some evil to happen to you? How did you respond? How should we respond?

9. As things get worse, Arissa just tries harder to protect Charity on her own and gain some sense of control over the situation. Have you ever felt this way? How did you respond? What would you have done differently from Arissa?

10. Arissa has been trying to protect Charity on her own strength, but she has to learn how to completely trust God instead. What does she learn about herself and her heavenly Father? What impact does that have on the choices she makes at the end?

11. When Arissa tells Nathan that she trusts him completely, he responds with a strong emotional reaction (and a sizzling

kiss!). Why did her words mean so much to him? How did her words change his thoughts or attitude?

12. Arissa's theme verse is Psalm 40:2, 3: "He lifted me out of the slimy pit; out of the mud and mire; He set my feet on a rock and gave me a firm place to stand. He put a new song in my mouth, a hymn of praise to our God. Many will see and fear the Lord and put their trust in Him." What does that verse mean for you?

REQUEST YOUR FREE BOOKS!

2 FREE RIVETING INSPIRATIONAL NOVELS IN TRUE LARGE PRINT PLUS 2 FREE MYSTERY GIFTS

Love Inspired®
SUSPENSE

TRUE LARGE PRINT

YES! Please send me 2 FREE Love Inspired® Suspense True Large Print novels and my 2 FREE mystery gifts (gifts are worth about $10). After receiving them, if I don't wish to receive any more books, I can return the shipping statement marked "cancel." If I don't cancel, I will receive 3 brand-new true large print novels every month and be billed just $7.99 per book in the U.S. or $9.99 per book in Canada. That's a savings of at least 33% off the cover price. It's quite a bargain! Shipping and handling is just 50¢ per book in the U.S. and 75¢ per book in Canada.* I understand that accepting the 2 free books and gifts places me under no obligation to buy anything. I can always return the shipment and cancel at any time. Even if I never buy another book, the two free books and gifts are mine to keep forever.

124/324 IDN FV2K

Name _____ (PLEASE PRINT)

Address _____ Apt. # _____

City _____ State/Prov. _____ Zip/Postal Code _____

Signature (if under 18, a parent or guardian must sign) _____

Mail to the **Harlequin® Reader Service:**
IN U.S.A.: P.O. Box 1867, Buffalo, NY 14240-1867
IN CANADA: P.O. Box 609, Fort Erie, Ontario L2A 5X3

* Terms and prices subject to change without notice. Prices do not include applicable taxes. Sales tax applicable in N.Y. Canadian residents will be charged applicable taxes. Offer not valid in Quebec. This offer is limited to one order per household. Not valid for current subscribers to Love Inspired Suspense True Large Print books. All orders subject to credit approval. Credit or debit balances in a customer's account(s) may be offset by any other outstanding balance owed by or to the customer. Please allow 4 to 6 weeks for delivery. Offer available while quantities last.

Your Privacy—The Harlequin® Reader Service is committed to protecting your privacy. Our Privacy Policy is available online at www.ReaderService.com or upon request from the Harlequin Reader Service.

We make a portion of our mailing list available to reputable third parties that offer products we believe may interest you. If you prefer that we not exchange your name with third parties, or if you wish to clarify or modify your communication preferences, please visit us at www.ReaderService.com/consumerschoice or write to us at Harlequin Reader Service Preference Service, P.O. Box 9062, Buffalo, NY 14269. Include your complete name and address.

ReaderService.com

Manage your account online!

- Review your order history
- Manage your payments
- Update your address

> ### We've designed the Harlequin® Reader Service website just for you.

Enjoy all the features!

- Reader excerpts from any series
- Respond to mailings and special monthly offers
- Discover new series available to you
- Browse the Bonus Bucks catalogue
- Share your feedback

Visit us at:

ReaderService.com